THE HAUNTING OF HARRINGTON HOUSE

MARIE WILKENS

PROLOGUE

"Now is the time," Josiah whispered. "If we wait any longer, then he might change the will."

Patrick shook his head, his eyes moving from his brother to the study door on the other side of the room. No matter what Josiah thought, the old man had hearing like a bat. He could probably hear them despite being asleep a half dozen doors down from where they were speaking. Josiah rolled his eyes and slouched back in the lavish leather chair. They had only been back at their childhood home for two days, yet the tension was already evident whenever they were in the same room as the old man.

"You know it's going to happen, mark my words. Sooner or later, he's going to go off the handle and make sure neither of us sees a dime of his money. We need to do something, and you know it."

"Yeah, I know it," Patrick grumbled. "I also know he locks his doors, and you don't have the balls to follow through with your little plan. I'll be left cleaning up the mess like always, and I'm not going to have his blood on my hands."

Josiah leaned forward, intrigued, it seemed, by his brother for the first time. Patrick realized the error of his ways. He had opened the door for the discussion, a dangerous game to be playing with a man who was out for blood.

"What if I told you that you didn't have to do anything? All you had to do was be there and keep your mouth shut?" Josiah asked.

"If you think it's something you can do, then you shouldn't need me there at all," Patrick said.

"No, no, you have to be there, too. If we don't do it together, then how do I know you won't take the money and turn me in?"

Patrick scoffed. "I am insulted that you would even insinuate it. I would never turn on my brother, my flesh and blood."

"Be that as it may, if I am going to do this for us, brother, then I need you to bear witness as well."

Patrick sat back, intrigued for the first time by his brother's proposition. It didn't seem as though he was going to make any progress in trying to dissuade Josiah from his plan. No matter how close Josiah got to that point, Patrick was almost certain that his brother could never go through with the horrific act.

He was simply talking a big game as he always did. For once, Patrick was going to call him on his shenanigans.

"All right, Josiah. If you want to do this, then we do it tonight, right now. Let's see you put your money where your mouth is."

His brother paled some, the smile falling from his face, but to Patrick's surprise, Josiah straightened himself in the chair. His shoulders stiffened, his chest filling with air as he nodded to his brother and stood up. It seemed as though Josiah was not going to let Patrick win so easily, but Patrick wasn't swayed by his brother's bravado. He knew Josiah was all talk and no action. It had been the same way their entire lives, ever since they were little children.

Even now, as he stood to follow Josiah, his heart racing with excitement, Patrick didn't expect anything to happen. He had seen his brother line up the old man in the sight of his gun before while they were out hunting. The perfect accident had been laid out for him on a silver platter, and Josiah would freeze at that pivotal moment. They crept through the massive house, the most beautiful manor in the state, without making a single sound. Carefully, they moved, hearts pounding at the thrill of being caught by the staff in their torrid act. When they reached the family patriarch's door, Josiah gave Patrick a wink before turning the knob slowly and slipping inside.

Together, they silently moved, one to each side of

the sleeping man's bed. Even in his aged state, there was a fear buried deep inside of Patrick. He knew what his father was capable of, and if he wasn't stopped, their family's fortune would be nothing but pennies. While others saw his charitable work and praised the man, his own sons saw it and watched in horror as the coffers were drained. In the last few months, he'd spoken in depth about leaving it all to a worthy soul, though Patrick had no idea what the crazed man could mean. His breath caught in his chest as Josiah picked up a pillow from the bed and held it above their father's sleeping form.

"Once you start, you know you can't stop, right? He'll never forgive you if he makes it. You'll spend the rest of your life behind bars," Patrick whispered.

"Don't tell me you're the one having second thoughts now," Josiah said.

Patrick rolled his eyes. "Let's get out of here. We both know you're not going to do anything, and if he wakes up and catches us, we'll be disowned for sure."

"No, brother. No running away this time. I'm done living in his shadow…"

Suddenly, the expression on his brother's face shifted from one of playful yet dark humor to a look that sent a chill down Patrick's spine. Josiah's gaze was cold as the smile fell from his lips. Slowly, his eyes moved to their father. Before Patrick could register what was about to happen, Josiah shoved the pillow down over their father's head forcefully, holding the man down as he thrashed against the sudden fight for his life. Patrick, in a hushed whisper, pleaded with his brother to stop, begging him to see the mistake they were making, but it was already too late. As the man stopped fighting beneath Josiah, Patrick struggled to catch his breath.

"Josiah," he whispered. "Josiah, what have you done?"

The man smiled, dark and menacing. "I've set us free, brother. Free from this prison once and for all…"

1

*A*nna Bowman was sitting in the back of their traveling van, trying to finish the blog she had been working on throughout the day. Her friend, Emily Garrett, whom she had met three years before, was driving. They had originally met at a meet and greet for other social influencers and became best friends. The two of them had been traveling the country together, living the van lifestyle to the best of their abilities for the last year and a half. As far as she could tell, they both thoroughly enjoyed everything they shared, and the fact that she had found someone who was just like her made life feel so much easier. While Anna had found her niche as a true crime and ghost story novelist, Emily sided more with murder and mysteries.

Her friend had originally gone to college to study journalism, but after a short time trying to make a living with that, something had drawn her to writing fiction novels. Anna definitely didn't mind, since it was something else they had in common. On top of writing her own novels and sharing her driving duties, Emily also ran a fan site and a blog of her own. Both of them had come from different lifestyles growing up, but it certainly didn't change the fact they adored each other. She knew the moment they met, but since they had been traveling together, she had grown to understand how close they were as friends.

While it wasn't always easygoing, she wouldn't trade it for anything. Anna and Emily were both bloggers and novelists, but she was pretty sure that whether or not they became bestsellers, nothing about their lives was going to change other than the fact that they would be famous. Even if that did happen, she hoped it wouldn't change much about what they were doing. She had grown up in the foster care system and was constantly in and out of several homes throughout her teenage years. If she had to pick a reason she had become a writer, it was because of the awful things she had been through all those years ago. Even at twenty-six, she had yet to get over everything she had seen growing up the way she did.

Anna wasn't bothered by what her past had taught her, but it was in the back of her mind more than she felt like it should have been. Several of the thoughts going through her head were causing her to struggle as she tried to finish up the last of the blog. Anna was just about done when the van bounced after hitting a pothole, causing her and her laptop to be tossed into the air. When she crashed down and looked toward the front of the van, Emily was already glancing at her in the mirror and apologizing. She simply chuckled, pulled her computer back onto her lap, and continued typing. Although she wasn't necessarily in a hurry to get the blog posted, she kept to a certain schedule so her readers didn't have to wait long for what she had written.

Once she was able to push all other thoughts from her mind, she managed to almost finish the work she had been doing. At the very least, she managed to finish her line of thinking and get it typed into her document before she lost it. Anna closed her laptop and placed it into the bag at her feet before climbing between the seats and into the passenger seat. It wasn't until she was sitting down that she realized Emily was pulling up to a picturesque campground, one they had decided on earlier that day. They were somewhere around Harrington, Louisiana, which was an area they had not been to since they had started traveling together. She had always felt that the best thing about the way they traveled was the fact that they got to see several new places every week, and she loved the view and colorfulness of it all. As soon as they came to a stop at the security booth, a man in a worn-out uniform approached the driver's side.

"Are you guys Emily and Anna?" he asked.

Emily nodded. "That would be us."

"I just need to see your ID and get a picture of your license plate before I let you onto the property. I will also give you a pamphlet with a list of our rules."

"We appreciate it."

They both pulled out their IDs and signed a form when the man came back from his booth. Overall, Anna was impressed with the location and was happy to see they took security seriously. No matter how much they enjoyed traveling the country and living in their van, there were times when bad things would happen. More than once, they had been a few camping spots away from a break-in or an argument, and after the first time they had witnessed something of that nature, the two of them agreed to make sure they had researched the campgrounds a little better before their arrival. As the man handed them their IDs back and pointed them toward the secluded spot they had picked, the two of them smiled and thanked him before heading deeper into the campground.

Anna hadn't even seen the location they had chosen in person, but she was already planning on giving them a five-star review based solely on how they handled the entrance to the campground. Her blog was filled with reviews for places all over the country, and she knew there were thousands of people interested in the locations she and her friend had seen. It was part of the beauty of the lifestyle they had chosen, and she wouldn't change things in her life. As they pulled up to the secluded spot and Emily parked the van, she knew they had made the right choice about staying in that particular location.

Once they were parked and ready to settle in, they both set up the area outside of the van. They had prepared their camping area so many times that they could practically do it with their eyes closed, and it didn't take them long to finish setting up their camper and outdoor awning they had purchased a few months before. It was one of the best investments they had made on their journey, and she loved the fact that they finally had something covering the entrances to both the camper and the van, knowing the weather didn't always cooperate with what they were trying to do.

As soon as they finished setting up, Emily went to work on her blog while Anna prepared the grill. It was one of her favorite parts of the day, knowing they would simply be able to enjoy the area around them. Every once in a while, they would splurge on steaks or pork chops, but that day was a simple meal. After the grill was up to temperature, she tore open a package of hot dogs and threw them on the fire. Although both of them were enjoying their place for the night, she was already thinking about their next destination. Anna was well aware of how good her life was, and she couldn't imagine traveling the country without her best friend by her side.

It didn't take long for the hot dogs to finish cooking, and she pulled them off of the grill and put them on a plate before heading to the picnic table that sat just off to the side of their camp. Emily was sitting at the table, working on her blog, and Anna had already placed her laptop on the table when they first started setting up their camp. Anna smiled, watching Emily twirl a small blue piece of worn glass between her fingers. Long ago, when they had first met, Emily explained to Anna that the glass was the last piece of a windshield from her great-grandfather's Impala.

It was a reminder to her of how precious life was. Though she came from money, her great-grandfather had instilled in her a sense of adventure from a young age. The stone, to hear Emily tell the story, had saved her life on numerous occasions through bouts of depression. Those days were long behind her now. Life couldn't get any better, and it was nice to have the perfect person to share it all with. While they ate and talked about their work, Emily was working on her own blog, and Anna couldn't help but do some research on her computer. Before she could get very far into her own research, Emily suddenly turned her computer around and grinned.

"Check out this old auction site I found," Emily said.

"What is that? I thought you were working on your blog."

"I am, but you know how much I like to check out

things like this when we are in a new area. I spotted this old mansion, and I immediately thought about you. I know your love for mystery and hauntings."

"Well, I can't deny that."

"That's exactly what I was thinking," Emily said. "Before you say anything, just take a look at a few of these pictures."

2

Anna smiled, knowing her friend was accurate about the fact that she would enjoy what she was seeing. The creepy old mansion that sat in the photograph in the middle of the laptop screen was unusual in more ways than one. With several of the stories she had written in the past about hunting ghosts and spirits, she could almost see the history pouring out of the image on the screen. Although Anna was well aware of why Emily had decided to show her the picture, she had no idea why it was calling to her. There was almost a sadness to the photograph, and she couldn't quite place where it was coming from. There was something about the mansion pulling her attention to it.

"It has a beauty of its own, but what am I supposed to be looking at here?" Anna asked.

Emily smiled. "It's on an auction website. The

mansion is rumored to have a hidden treasure somewhere inside."

"You know stuff like that is a scam, right?"

"I don't think this one is. I know I was supposed to be working on my blog, but once this link popped up and I got a good look at the pictures of the mansion, I couldn't resist digging into it a little more."

Anna sighed. "All right, you have my attention for just a few minutes. Tell me what you found while you were doing your research."

"We could get the mansion for a steal."

"Now I know this whole thing is nothing more than a scam. I bet they have it at some crazy-low price, and now it is in your interest. You have to stop doing things like this to yourself."

Emily laughed. "You're partially right, but I have done a little research on it to see what I could find and if the house does have a history."

"Aside from the fact that you think that you can get this mansion at a historically low price, what makes you so interested in it?"

"It's just a creepy old mansion that caught my eye, but the history I have read so far is intriguing. I was only reading because the auction was listed rather strangely."

"What do you mean by that?"

"Instead of actually having a listing price or a goal for purchase, they had it listed at one hundred dollars. When I clicked on the link, I started to read the description, and I found out they were actually selling tickets. Each ticket is one hundred dollars, and they are only selling five thousand of them."

"So basically, they are raffling the mansion off instead of trying to sell it, since they know they are never going to get that much for it ."

"Pretty much, but I wanted you to get a good look at it as well because they are almost sold out of tickets."

Anna laughed. "Just judging by the outside of that house, I doubt the place is even worth a third of the total ticket sales."

"Yeah, but we only have to buy one at the low price of one hundred dollars to get it. Not only would we have a mansion we could call our own, but we would have a chance at finding the fortune that no one else has ever been able to locate."

"Look, it's kind of an awesome place just because of how creepy it is, but even at a hundred dollars, that's too rich for my blood."

"I'm telling you, this place has some good bones and could be something we could call home or simply fix up a bit and turn around to make it profit."

"You're more than welcome to buy a ticket if you want to, but I'm out."

Emily had a playful scowl on her face before she dove back into the screen on her laptop. As much as Anna loved Emily and all the things they enjoyed doing together, there was no way that Anna would be willing to put any money toward a mansion that wasn't worth a dime. She enjoyed the lifestyle they had been living over the past year and a half, and she wasn't ready to take a chance on something that was going to cost them a fortune to rebuild. Even if her friend was writing about some secret treasure hidden in the house, she knew their chances of winning were almost zero. The last thing she needed was a worthless piece of property.

Although she was trying to get back to work and some of the research she needed to do before they headed to their next location, Anna was struggling to focus. She looked out over the campground, trying to find something that would start a fire in her writing process, but nothing was coming to her. Instead, she thought about her life and what had led her to become the person she was. She was never the type of person who would ever complain about the life she had or what she had been through, but she'd had it rough growing up. Being raised in the foster care system was something she wouldn't wish on anyone, but she knew her life was more successful than she was giving herself credit for.

There were times when she was a teenager when she felt like she was going to give up, and even though that time never came to fruition, she thought about it regularly. Before she found her passion, Anna had struggled to find a purpose in life. By the time she was fourteen, just before starting high school, she had already been through seven different foster families. There was a time in her life when she thought she was the problem and the reason no one wanted her. It wasn't until she was a little older that she realized how hard it was for the families who were trying to help raise her.

Anna finally did some of her own research on the computer a few years later and started to understand how difficult the process was for families working in the foster care system. She had never caused any trouble with any of the people she stayed with, but she had always felt like she was more trouble than she was worth. It wasn't until one of her teachers took an interest in her and showed her the magic of reading that she began to focus on writing. If it hadn't been for that one teacher at the beginning of high school, Anna had no idea where she would be at that moment.

As she stared out past their camp and into a wooded area not far beyond it, she realized how lucky she was. Anna could hear Emily typing beside her as she finished the last few bites of her hot dog. There wasn't anyone who would ever be able to tell her that her life wasn't perfect, and she was happy she was getting the chance to share it all with her best friend.

Knowing it was just a matter of time before one of them would finally gain the success they had been looking for, Anna took a deep breath and sighed before getting back to work on her laptop. Anna spent the next half an hour splitting her time between a haunting story she had been working on and the blog she needed to share with her readers. In that short amount of time, she had managed to get quite a bit done. She posted the blog to her website and sat back, waiting for the views to start rolling in.

When she had originally set up the blog and started to actually get some followers, she had no idea what she was doing. Luckily for her, several of her followers started to show her the ropes. Anna thought about how hard the industry was supposed to be to break into, and even though she wasn't one of the most well-known bloggers across the world, there were a lot of people who loved to hear what she had to say. Good or bad, it didn't change how she felt about what she had done with her life, but she couldn't wait for the day when one of her novels would take off and rise through the sales charts. She was well aware of the fact that she was simply daydreaming about what could be eventually, but as she sat quietly, waiting for Emily to finish whatever work she had left to do, Anna knew someday it would become a reality.

3
―――

Anna was pretty sure that the majority of writers across the world understood her feelings and passion. While many writers would never make it in the industry, they had stories to tell. She could remember when she first started writing and trying to understand the process. It didn't take her long to understand why there were so many levels that novels needed to pass through. While the writer might have something in particular in mind, an editor or someone else through the process might see it from a different point of view. It was almost magical to watch a novel make its way up through the ranks of the industry, even if a lot of them fell flat.

Shaking the memories and thoughts from her mind, she stared at her screen for several moments before she heard a chime coming from her speakers, indicating a new e-mail. She wondered what her readers were already trying to tell her. Just as she started to reach her hand toward the trackpad, she also heard Emily giggling from across the table. Instead of thinking about her followers, she was curious about what her friend was up to next. The woman was always messing around and playing pranks, and she could only imagine what she had done.

Anna wondered what kind of shenanigans Emily was up to, and Anna knew the only way to find out was to open the e-mail that had just come through. With a smile on her face, she clicked on the application and watched all of her most recent emails pop up on her screen. The one at the very top had a generic address from where it had been sent, but she clicked on it, nonetheless. When the file opened and she saw her name at the top, she knew Emily had purchased one of the tickets she had been talking about for the mansion raffle. There was a copy of another e-mail sent right after from Emily. The woman had purchased two tickets.

Anna chuckled. "I told you I didn't want anything to do with it. The whole thing is a scam, and I can't believe you just fell for it."

"I'm glad we've known each other long enough for me to understand that you aren't being mean right now."

"I'm not trying to be mean, but I think this is a waste of time and money."

"I'm asking you to trust me," Emily replied. "I know a couple of hundred sounds like a lot of money right now, but we do have a slight chance of actually having our tickets pulled."

Anna sighed. "I suppose you're right. It would be kind of cool if we won and had the mansion all to ourselves."

"To hell with the mansion. As awesome as it would be to have the opportunity to live in a place like that with so much history, I'm thinking about the possibility of a lost treasure that has never been found inside. Can you imagine us winning and actually finding it?"

"I think you're getting a little ahead of yourself."

"Maybe, but I think that's what life should be about. Taking chances and hoping for the best outcome is the only way to live. I certainly wasn't about to put my own name in the hat without doing the same thing for you."

Anna laughed. "It's nice to know you were thinking about me. I tell you what. If I happen to have the winning ticket, I'll split the house with you."

"I was thinking the same thing if I win. I couldn't imagine living in a place like that without having my best friend there."

Anna knew they had grown closer over the years they had known each other, but it would feel strange to have a project so big and not have her friend by her side. Emily was her best friend in the world, and if it wasn't for her, she had no idea how far she would have made it on her own. It was strange to feel the excitement was starting to build up inside. Although she had written about old mansions and hauntings in the past, the thought of actually owning a place she could write about was like something straight from a dream. She started to think about the pictures her friend had shown her and decided to look up the site that had the auction listed.

Emily was smiling. Anna was doing the same thing, and the two of them sat silently across from each other, each off in their own little world. Anna was thinking about all the possibilities that would come from owning a mansion of that stature, even if it did need a ton of work. As she scrolled through the pictures posted on the website, she realized there weren't very many that included the inside of it. For several moments, she thought about what the interior of the mansion looked like and what kind of stories would come from seeing it all firsthand.

Although it was a long shot that either one of them would have their ticket pulled for ownership, she couldn't help but think about the possibilities. Anna wasn't even sure if she could give up the traveling life, knowing how much they both loved it. A part of her wondered what it would be like to have a place to call home. It wasn't until she started to read the description that she realized the mansion was actually just down the road from them. The address on file was only about twenty miles from the campground where they were staying the night, and the drawing for the mansion was the next day.

"I think we should stay at the campground for another night, at least until they draw the ticket tomorrow," Emily said.

Anna nodded. "I just noticed the address is not far from here, but I don't think we are going to win anything."

"That's the excitement of it all. I feel like if we expected to win, then it's no longer any fun. I know this whole thing is a long shot, but you're a writer, just like me. We need to allow ourselves to fantasize about dreams like this every once in a while."

"I can't argue with that logic."

"Of course you can't," Emily replied with a smile. "I think we should make a little party out of it. We can get a little alcohol for tomorrow night and enjoy the evening while we wait for the drawing."

Anna chuckled softly, but she nodded in agreement. Staying for just one more day wasn't going to make any difference since they lived their lives on the road anyway. It was hard to argue with Emily's enthusiasm, and Anna could actually feel excitement starting to creep up inside as well. She wasn't sure if it was because she never had anywhere to call home before or if it was simply Emily starting to rub off on her. Either way, her mind was already starting to create plans for something she had no information about other than the fact that she was the owner of a ticket that could possibly lead to her ownership of the mansion.

They both stayed outside and sat at the picnic table for another hour, playing on their computers. She had no idea what Emily was doing on her own laptop, but she was so fascinated with the mansion that she was trying to find any historical information she could. When she finally found a website that might give her answers to the questions she had, Anna had to slap her arm and kill a mosquito that had just landed on her. It didn't take long for the sun to go down and the mosquitoes to take over, and before she had the opportunity to dig any deeper into her research, it was time to go inside the camper. The camper was a small but cozy one, and it had just enough room for the two of them to sleep comfortably. After they had both settled in for the night and she closed her eyes, she started to doze off while thinking about the mansion and all the things they could do with it.

4

Anna awoke early the next morning, and Emily wasn't far behind. They went through their morning routine, and it wasn't long before both of them were sitting outside, enjoying the cooler air that came with it being before noon. It was already late July, and the nights were warmer than normal. Being in Louisiana wasn't much help, considering it had already gotten to record highs that summer. The two of them were both working on their novels, along with blogging everything they had done up to that point. She was excited about the possibility of winning the drawing for the mansion, but she was even more excited about sharing the news with all of their followers.

While she normally tried to keep her blogs at a certain word count, there were times when Anna would simply drop a few quick comments to keep her followers updated. The website they use to get their blogs off the ground was shared by both of them, although they each had a separate account to use and post through. Emily could see everything Anna was sharing with the group, and so could she when it came to anything that her friend posted. As soon as she had finished letting all of her followers know they would be staying at the campground for an extra day, waiting for the raffle, she started to dig through the internet to find as much information about the old place as she could.

Even though she had found a website the night before, she was hopeful it would give her some answers she was looking for, but it turned out to be nothing more than a website used to spread rumors. There were several stories on the web page she ignored, even if they did make for good entertainment. Finally, after what felt like hours of digging through link after link, she gave up on the idea that she was going to be able to find any information about the so-called treasure her friend was talking about. While there were several links that talked about some hidden treasure in the mansion, there was nothing substantial she could base a good opinion on.

Anna eventually gave up and started to go back to work on her novel. Over the next couple of hours, she was able to get more work done than she had first expected. She was surprised when she closed her laptop and saw that Emily was already sitting across from her with her hands folded on the table. It wasn't very often they both completed their work at the same time, but Anna was already looking forward to the chance they were about to receive to get a look at the town of Harrington. The small amount of information she was able to find on the internet about the town was small and contained only around fifteen hundred residents. It made sense, given the area they were in and how far it seemed to be from any of the major cities, but she was looking forward to driving the twenty miles there and seeing it firsthand.

Anna had been working on her novel for several hours and hadn't even noticed that Emily had already disconnected the van from the camper and had them ready to take off as soon as she was finished working. They both climbed into the van and headed south in the direction of the small town. As they approached the small town they were looking for, Emily had planned on driving by the location of the mansion where she had purchased the raffle tickets. She slowed down the van as they approached the front gates, which she could only assume led to the mansion. Anna noticed the black iron gates. It almost looked like something out of a horror story, and she smiled.

"It's much larger than I expected it to be, but it's always hard to tell from pictures," Emily said.

Anna nodded. "It's every bit as creepy as the

pictures made it seem. It would be a perfect little place to sit and write for days on end."

"So, you are a little excited about the possibility of owning this place?"

Anna chuckled. "More than I should be, that's for sure. I just wish I could have found a little more information on it. The only thing I found on the internet seemed to be nothing more than rumors told by the people who have passed through."

"That's the same thing I was thinking. Is it just me, or do those black gates make the place seem more ominous?"

"I don't know, but I can think of a ton of different things we can do with the property and the rest of the estate. I bet there is some sort of story we could learn that would draw a crowd here."

Emily smiled. "I haven't thought about that, but you bring up a good point."

Anna simply nodded and smiled before turning her attention back to the mansion behind the iron gates. Although she had only seen it in pictures up to that point, there was something about it that brought some familiarity to it. It was hard to shake the feeling that there was something darker behind the gates, but she was pulled from her thoughts when she heard a quick blip from a police cruiser. Turning around, she noticed what seemed to be a local cop pulling up behind them. She wondered what they had done wrong, and even though Emily had brought the van to a stop at the side of the road, in front of the property, they weren't breaking any laws. It didn't take long for the officer to climb out of his patrol car and make his way up to the driver's side window as her friend slowly rolled it down.

"I'm going to have to ask the two of you to keep it moving," he said.

"Are we doing anything wrong?"

"Not necessarily, but you are partially pulled into the driveway of this old place, which means you are trespassing. You're either going to have to keep it moving, or I'm going to have to ticket you for the infraction."

Emily smiled. "There's no need for that. We simply saw the gates and the old mansion in the background. We just thought we would take a quick peek and nothing more."

"Well, you've had your look, and I don't feel like writing either one of you a ticket. So, as long as you start to pull away before I get back to my cruiser, I think we will all be happy."

Emily thanked the officer for giving them a fair warning and immediately started to roll the window up as he started to walk away. Glancing back at her, she couldn't hold back the laugh she had been holding in. They were shaking their heads and laughing together as Emily put the van back into drive and started to pull away. Within just a few moments, they pulled into the small village of Harrington and noticed a sign for an antique shop in the middle of town. As they slowly started to drive past the building, Anna was disappointed by the fact that the shop was closed. One of her favorite things to do as they drove around the country was to stop at any of the antique shops they found and take a look around. She had found several small trinkets during their journey, and she loved spending hours looking around old antique shops anytime they came across one.

Within a few minutes of passing the shop, Emily pulled the van into the parking lot of a small grocery store on the other end of town. It appeared to be owned by someone local and not one of the big chain stores all over the country, but Anna loved supporting local businesses. Anytime she had the chance, she would much rather use her money to support local shops. They headed inside to grab some wine and snacks for the small party they were throwing for themselves, all the while talking about all the things they could do with the mansion if they won it. The only idea they both seemed to share was that it would make a great place for a bed and breakfast, but there were other ideas thrown around, such as creating a haven for aspiring writers to visit. Either way, she was growing more excited with every passing moment.

5

Hours later, they were back at the campground and enjoying what they both considered a day off. As a writer, she always had the option to take any day off she wanted. It was rare that Anna would go an entire day without doing some kind of work, and although she had already done some that morning, she was far too excited to get anything done when they returned. Instead, they spent some time roaming the campgrounds and getting a better look at the area. It was something they always did when they found a campground they both enjoyed, and it also gave them more information they could share with their followers, who were looking for ideal places to camp. While her blog was informational for other campers, it was also where she spent most of her time promoting their novels.

Anna knew that having another writer by her side motivated her to keep going on a daily basis. While the two of them wrote in different genres and styles, it was always the friendly competition to finish a book that would push her the hardest. As Emily handed her another glass of wine, Anna couldn't help but think about the idea that they could be moments away from owning a mansion they had never heard of before. The closest they had come to seeing what the place looked like was when they had driven by earlier that day, and that was more than enough to get her creative juices flowing. She had already made several moves throughout the day to remind herself of things she wanted to put in her next novel.

"What do you think our chances are of actually winning this drawing?" Emily asked.

Anna chuckled. "About one in twenty-five hundred. I mean, we bought two tickets out of the five thousand sold. I'd say we don't stand a chance at all."

"That's fair, but it's exciting to think about, isn't it?"

"You got me there. It's hard not to feel something when you are looking at it like that. I wonder what the inside of the place looks like and if it is in as bad a shape as the outside, but I think it would make a perfect bed and breakfast."

Emily smiled. "I can't help but think the same

thing. Can you imagine having a place like that where we could serve breakfast and have a place for writers like us to stay? It's such a remote and beautiful location, aside from the darkness that seems to be surrounding it."

Anna nodded. "I thought I was the only one who felt that, but I can't help but think that the place is calling me somehow. There's almost something familiar about it."

"I don't know about any of that, but it would be amazing to have a place that is all of our own."

Anna tilted her head. "Is the van and camper not big enough for you anymore?"

Emily chuckled. "Trust me, it's perfect just the way it is. It's nice to think we have a chance to actually have a place to call home."

Anna and her friend were made to find each other. They had so much in common that there were times each of them would finish each other's sentences. Knowing they both wanted a place to call home was just another goal they shared, but the chances of them actually winning the raffle were slim to none. Anna heard something on the television behind them and turned around just in time to catch the small-town mayor starting to speak. The little town never gained much attention, since the mayor seemed to be a mixture of excited and nervous at the same time. They had nearly finished a bottle of wine before the announcement even started, but Emily had gotten up and moved the television so they could see it from the picnic table under the awning. When her friend turned and chuckled in her direction, she figured they were thinking the same thing once again.

"Can you imagine how much publicity this small town is getting because of this whole thing? It has to be a huge financial help for the entire town."

Anna nodded. "I can only imagine. A place like this that is so far off the map that I'm sure hardly anyone even knows exists could use all the publicity it can get his hands on."

"He seems pretty nervous."

"I was thinking the same thing. I'm sure there aren't many times he gets to talk to the media."

They both nodded at the same time and turned their attention back to the screen when the mayor of Harrington introduced a woman they had never seen. The woman had a huge smile on her face as she approached the podium, which had obviously been built just for the drawing. She introduced herself as the community's financial advisor and told them they had sold quite a few of the available tickets. Anna was fascinated with the entire process unfolding on the television, since she had never seen anything like it.

Anna could tell the event was a big thing for the community when they spent the next thirty minutes making all sorts of announcements and carrying on with other festivities. The situation reminded her of a small-town fair being held, but in the amount of time it had taken them to reach the conclusion of the raffle drawing, Anna and Emily had downed several more glasses of wine, finishing a bottle they had purchased in town earlier that day. All the tickets were in a medium-sized cage, and the mayor spun them around several times before opening a small door and the woman started to reach inside. Anna could feel her heart start to race with anticipation, even though the odds were not in their favor.

Everything was unfolding on the television screen, which seemed to be moving in slow motion. When the woman finally pulled a ticket from inside the cage and held it up, Anna suddenly felt like she had won it all. It was almost like she had someone whispering in her ear, telling her how important she was and she deserved all the good things in life she had missed out on. A chill ran up her spine just before the winning number was read off. Anna and Emily were staring at their computer screens as the woman read the number of the winning ticket. Immediately, she jumped up from the picnic table with excitement.

"That's my number," Anna exclaimed.

"No way. Are you serious? You just won the mansion?"

Anna could only muster enough strength to nod. She couldn't believe she had actually won the raffle and she was going to be the new owner of the creepy mansion. It was hard to believe that what she thought was a scam had turned out to be quite the opposite, but she didn't have a chance to let anything sink in, since Emily had already closed the distance between them and jumped into her arms. Both of them were jumping up and down, holding each other tightly. Although they had each come from different backgrounds, both of them were just as excited as the other to have finally won something of such significance.

Once it actually registered that she was the winner, Anna glanced over at the television screen to see a phone number scrolling across the bottom. The winning ticket holder was asked to call the number to set up an appointment in order to collect the winnings, and she reached for her phone and typed in the number. They were both celebrating when a woman on the other end of the line answered with just as much excitement in her voice as she was feeling. She was surprised that the only thing that needed to be done was to make everything official. By meeting with the mayor and the financial advisor the following morning, Anna would be given the keys once the paperwork had been signed.

As soon as she heard the call, Anna looked at Emily, who was staring back at her. Neither one of them could believe what had just happened, but she was the new owner of an old mansion. Emily poured more wine for both of them, and they clanked their glasses together before taking another drink. It was impossible for her to wrap her head around what had just happened, but the only thing she knew for sure was they were going to get all the information they needed the next morning. For now, Anna knew the only thing they could do was celebrate their winning and dream about the plans they were already thinking about for the property.

6

Anna was well beyond tipsy by the time she lay down that night, and although she was thinking nothing but happy thoughts as she went to sleep, her dreams didn't seem to share the same amount of joy. Instead of dreaming about all the things they could do with the property and mansion, she tossed and turned all night with terrible nightmares running through her mind. When she woke up the next morning, she felt just as exhausted as she had the night before when she had first lain down. The entire night had been filled with nightmares about the house and someone chasing her through it, even if she had no idea what the interior even looked like. It was one of the strangest things she could ever remember dreaming, but it didn't take long for her to forget them when she realized what the day would entail.

The day before had started out as any other, with them heading to a new location to scope out. Anna was happy they had made the stop and even more excited that her friend hadn't listened to her and had purchased the tickets anyway. She knew if it wasn't for Emily buying a raffle ticket, they would have already been long gone from Harrington. Instead, they were packing up their things just like they always would but were only heading down the road and not to some other state. The happiness Anna felt and the joy she shared with Emily made her forget all the things she had dreamed about the night before.

Although they had developed a process over time to pack their things and head out each day, they somehow managed to work through the process quicker than they ever had before. In almost no time at all, they had everything put away and the camper hooked back up to the van. Within an hour of being awake and eating breakfast, they were back on the road. The only difference between that day and any other day was the fact that they were only going to be traveling about twenty miles south, and she was already looking forward to sitting down with the lawyer and signing all the paperwork to make the mansion theirs. They always took turns driving, and that day was her turn to take the wheel, even if they weren't going to be traveling all that far.

"Are we on the same page with making it a bed

and breakfast, along with the possibility of turning it into some sort of a resort for writers?" Emily asked.

Anna nodded. "I'm on board with the idea, but I'm not sure how we're going to be able to go forward with the construction to get everything up to code."

"I hadn't thought about that."

"There weren't a whole lot of pictures of the interior, either, so I have no idea how much work that is going to take."

"That's true. I bet we can get a loan for all the work that is going to need to be done. I'll message my dad and see what he says. How about getting a loan?"

Russ Garrett, Emily's father, was a very good man and a good father. Although Anna had never known her own parents, if she had been able to choose anyone to raise her, it would have been someone like him. He was one of her friend's biggest supporters and cheerleaders. In his eyes, Anna felt like Emily could do no wrong. To have a parent like him would have been one of her biggest dreams as a teenager, but it wasn't anything she held against the woman. They had both been raised in very different lives, and Anna was happy for the things she had and wouldn't change a thing, even if she could.

They had only been on the road for a couple of minutes up to that point, and she could already hear Emily's phone dinging with several messages. Although she had her eyes on the road, Anna knew her friend was messaging back and forth with her father. The chuckles she heard from Emily showed the man was obviously supportive of their plans. Just when they were within a few miles of the mansion and the estate was soon going to be signed over to them, Anna heard Emily exclaim and cheer with excitement.

"I take it that your dad is on board with what we want to do?"

Emily laughed. "He's excited about it. I think he's just as happy as we are right now, but he promised he would do whatever it took to make sure we got the loan."

"That's great. I wasn't even thinking that far ahead, but it's nice to know we are covered to take care of whatever we need to do on it."

"That's what I was thinking. I can't wait to see what this place is like inside. I'm excited."

Anna felt the same way, even if she was a little nervous about the whole thing. She had never owned something of such importance in her life. As far as things that mattered to her, the van was the closest thing to property that meant anything to her and even that was something she considered owning with her friend. They shared everything they owned, and she never thought twice about it at all. Knowing they were going to be owning the mansion together made the idea of owning an actual place to call home seem that much more comforting. It was a scary thought going through her mind, but it was outweighed by the excitement she was feeling about the situation in general.

Not only had she never owned anything before, but she had certainly never won anything so exciting in her life. The idea that she was actually going to own something she could live in and share with her best friend was the most important thing she was thinking about. While it was true that her life hadn't always had a happy ending, she was certainly hoping this time would be different. When they arrived at the mansion's front entrance, where they had seen the black gates closed the day before, she was surprised to find them wide open. As they started to pull in, she spotted two other cars sitting in the driveway. Anna brought the van to a stop, and the two of them climbed out. There were two people waiting for them with smiles on their faces, and she recognized them both from the television the night before.

"You must be the two young women we spoke to on the phone last night," the mayor said, shaking both of their hands. "This is a once-in-a-lifetime experience, and I'm happy we are getting the opportunity to meet the two of you. My name is Nancy Thomas, and this is Janice Snyder."

"It's a pleasure to meet you," Anna said.

They went around the group and shook hands before Janice pulled out a stack of paperwork for her to sign. Anna was staring up at the size of the mansion, having only seen it from the road before.

Even though it was going to need a ton of work before it would be ready for anything, she could see a hidden beauty beneath it all. She was already starting to look at the house from a different perspective than she had earlier that day, and she couldn't wait to get inside to get a better look around. The accountant handed her a pen, and she started to sign all the legal documents that would make the mansion hers and Emily's. She was so excited about the situation that she could feel the pen shaking in her hand, and she knew her nerves were starting to get the best of her.

"So, I can only imagine how surprising it was to hear your number read off, but I am curious if either of you have come up with any plans for the old mansion," Nancy said.

Emily smiled. "We have already kind of talked about the possibility of turning it into a bed and breakfast."

"That would be a wonderful addition to the area. It would be great for the town, and I can only imagine the number of people this place would draw to our area."

As Anna continued to sign the paperwork on the back of one of the cars that had been waiting for them, she couldn't help but listen to the conversation taking place behind her. From the sound of her voice, the mayor was just as excited about the possibility of a bed and breakfast as they were. She was looking forward to getting started as soon as possible. It didn't take long for her to complete the paperwork, and as soon as she initialed the last document, the mayor and the accountant handed her the keys, along with documentation that would prove her ownership. After several more smiles and goodbyes, Janice and Nancy climbed into their respective cars and pulled away, leaving her and Emily to take a look at their new home.

7

The two of them were standing in the driveway, looking up at the mansion in front of them. As excited as she was to get inside and to get a good look around, Anna was nervous about what they would find. The pictures had been well done, but they didn't give them a view of what they were getting themselves into. Either way, they were now the proud owners of a mansion for which they technically only spent two hundred dollars. There was nowhere in the world they would be able to purchase a place to live at that price, and she was excited about the next step in their adventure together. Nancy had handed her a flyer for the mansion with a list of the home's details, and she pulled it out to look as they headed toward the front door.

When they arrived at the front door to the

mansion, Anna hesitated for a moment, holding the key in her hand. The place had been built a long time ago, and she could tell by the carvings etched into the molding that went around the door frame. Taking a deep breath and exhaling slowly, she placed the key into the opening and turned the handle. A moment later, they were both stepping into the foyer of the mansion and although it was clearly going to take a lot of work to bring back the old glory it once carried, she could see all the beauty and possibilities in front of her. Although it was much larger than in a traditional home, it seemed to be designed with the same care and look as other homes she had seen in the past. It was a perfect place to set up the bed and breakfast they had talked about.

"Can you believe this place has six bedrooms?" Anna asked.

"Holy cow. I didn't think it was going to have that many, but then again, I'm not sure what I expected."

"According to the flyer, it is two floors and two rooms located in the twin peaks. Six bedrooms in total, with two of those rooms sharing a bathroom. The other four bedrooms have private bathrooms, and if that wasn't enough, there are two more bathrooms throughout the house for visitors to use."

Emily chuckled. "I never thought I would be in a house this big, let alone one that has that many bathrooms."

"I think I'm already excited about the kitchen."

"Let's start there."

They immediately started to follow the map, which had a rather cheap version of the layout of the home. With every step they took deeper into the center of the mansion, Anna was coming up with more ideas on how to lay out the bed and breakfast they were thinking about creating. As soon as they stepped foot into the kitchen, she was amazed by the sheer size of it. Not only was it larger than any kitchen she had been in before, but it opened up into a large greenhouse, which was slightly overgrown but beautiful, nonetheless. It was going to take some work to get things done and back into working order, but the thoughts going through her mind about the things they would be able to do were never-ending.

It took them some time to make their way through the mansion and get a feel for how to get around, but it seemed like everything had been designed in the perfect way for what they were already planning to do. Anna found herself even more curious about the estate's history, but there would be plenty of time to dive deeper into its past. As they made their way around, they found a small but very quaint library on the main floor, along with a living room, a dining room, and a drawing room. Although the few pictures on the website didn't show them very much at all, it was clearly more beautiful than she had anticipated.

By the time they finished checking out the second floor and finding two small sitting rooms, she was already starting to develop a plan for what she would want to see done with the place. The estate had much more potential than she had first thought, and Anna was looking forward to making all the plans with her best friend. Even though they hadn't gone through the entire house, the flyer stated that the mansion sat on twelve acres of land. It did state that four of those acres were overgrown but had been landscaped in the past. A large chunk of the property sat in a forest, which almost surrounded the house.

Anna and Emily spent a couple of hours making their way through the house and looking at all the woodwork throughout it. Although they had no idea how much time had passed, she realized what time it was when they finally arrived back down in the foyer. She was in shock by how much beauty could be seen throughout the house, and even though she looked forward to getting their new project started, there was a lot of work and research that would need to be done before any of the construction could be talked about. Emily was the first one to reach out and try to turn on one of the light switches, only to realize they didn't have any power.

"I suppose we should have known that already," Emily said.

Anna smiled. "This was mostly your idea, and you're the one who bought the tickets. You didn't think we would walk in here and everything would be up and running, did you?"

"No, but I'm not mad about spending that money. I just don't think it's a good idea we stay in here until we have the power on and are able to reach out to some contractors."

"I have no problem sleeping in the camper for the night. After all, I think we're both used to that by now. I do have to admit, it is going to be nice to have a place to call our own."

Emily smiled and nodded. "I'm looking forward to it, but it's going to take some time before that's a possibility. Maybe once we get the power turned on and get some things cleaned up, we'll be able to stay inside."

"I don't care. I'm excited about it all."

"Do you see all the potential that this place has?"

"Much more than I could see from the pictures, but I knew it had an aura that you would enjoy."

"I love it, but I'll love it a lot more once everything gets taken care of and we can get started on the construction."

"I'll e-mail my dad with some specifics, and we can start making phone calls in the morning to some contractors in the area," Emily said.

"I'll call around and see how we go about getting the power turned on. I think once we get it turned on and do some cleaning, we won't have any problems staying here throughout the night."

Emily just nodded and turned around to look around the room they were standing in. Although the house was more traditional than she had anticipated, Anna could see that there was plenty of hidden beauty beneath all of its cracks and flaws. She was hoping she would be able to find some sort of information that would lead to a possible way of promoting the bed and breakfast when it was completed. As long as there was a good story to tell, there was plenty of room to create a new sales pitch.

8

Anna and Emily spent the rest of that evening walking around the outskirts of the mansion and checking out the entirety of it all to the best of her ability. She didn't have any idea what else it was going to need, since she had no background in construction. A few of the things they added to the list immediately were roof and electrical work. Overall, she knew her friend had a good eye for what would make a perfect property to rebuild. Other than a lot of cosmetic work, it seemed as though the mansion itself had good bones, and she was already looking forward to seeing the final product once they were able to complete it all.

While they had plenty of odds and ends things to eat, they opted to head back into town and try the local pizza place. There were several people in the community who greeted them with smiles and congratulated them on winning, and Anna felt happier than she had in quite some time. Although she enjoyed the life she had been living with her best friend, the idea that they were going to be able to settle down in one location seemed like a perfect compromise. They talked about how they were going to get the bed and breakfast off the ground once the rebuilding was complete, and it would not only be a safe haven for visitors and writers but also a stream of income they didn't have before.

The rest of the evening passed by quietly and joyously as they celebrated their new home together. Anna couldn't wait until they had the power back on and she would be able to get a much better look around. What she looked forward to was the ability they would have to have a real roof over their heads. They talked until the sun went down about their plans before they each climbed into the small beds they had been sleeping in during their travels. Within just a few minutes, Anna could hear Emily snoring lightly right across from her, and it wasn't long before she was sleeping herself. She fell asleep thinking about all the excitement she had felt and how happy she was to share that excitement with her best friend.

Anna woke up the next morning when the sun was just starting to rise, and she felt more tired than she had the day before. All through the night, she tossed and turned while repeating the same strange dreams she'd had the night before. The only difference between the dreams the night before and the ones she'd had that night was the fact that she had finally seen the inside of the mansion. The nightmare that seemed to come and go all through the night was vivid in its details, but she shook any idea that they had meaning from her head. The only reason she was dreaming about the place was because of the excitement she had been going through.

Wiping the sleep from her eyes and noticing that her friend was asleep, she quietly got up and grabbed her camera. Anna wanted to get a head start on getting breakfast ready, but she also wanted to take a few pictures of their new property. As she opened the door to the camper and stepped outside, a waft of warm morning air hit her in the face. It was going to be another hot day in Louisiana, but she was looking forward to what the day would bring. It wasn't long after she stepped outside that she was cooking breakfast while snapping pictures of the property and the outside of the mansion. She wasn't sure she had ever had such a view to wake up to, and she couldn't wait until the entirety of the mansion had been remodeled.

With each photograph she took, she could see the plans for the house going through her mind. While it was hard to believe they actually owned the mansion and the estate that came with it, she had never thought she would own something so beautiful. The birds were chirping all around her, and there were a few squirrels running through the trees, which she had also taken pictures of. It was a beautiful morning to wake up to, but she couldn't shake the feeling that she was being watched. Even when she surveyed the area, she could see from the camper that no one was there.

The sensation in itself was a strange feeling, especially since she knew there was no one there besides her and Emily. Suddenly, all the sounds that the birds had been making grew silent. She couldn't quite tell what had caused it, but she had a sickness in the pit of her stomach she couldn't shake. After telling herself several times it was just morning jitters and trying to wake up from the bad dreams she'd had the night before, Anna set down the camera and focused on the eggs and bacon she had spent the morning preparing. It wasn't often she was up that much earlier than Emily, but she enjoyed the days she was able to get up and cook. Although Anna was enjoying the morning and smiling, the feeling in the pit of her stomach wouldn't go away. There was something watching her, but no matter how many times she tried to look for them, there was nothing there.

Without warning, the door to the camper swung open and made a loud sound when it smacked the side of the camper itself. Anna's heart was racing when she spun around. She chuckled when she realized that Emily was walking out. The woman gave her an awkward look, then simply smiled and shook her head before making her way down to one of the lawn chairs they had put up the night before when preparing their small campsite in front of the mansion. Once they both had about half a cup of coffee and were sharing breakfast, they started to try to figure out what they were going to do that day.

"You're going to have to get ahold of the power company today and see if we can get the electricity turned back on," Anna said.

Emily nodded. "I figured we would just make a list of contractors and all of that together, then split the list in half."

"That sounds perfect. I don't necessarily want to go with the cheapest one, but I also don't want to spend an arm and a leg on the place. It's going to need quite a bit of work."

"That's true, but if we do everything right, this place is going to make a perfect bed and breakfast."

"I can almost see it."

Emily smiled and went back to eating breakfast as the two of them continued their discussion. It was obvious by the tour of the mansion they had taken the day before that there was going to be a lot of work that needed to be done. Even though she was well aware of how much time and money it was going to take to complete the project, she could almost see what the house and everything around it was going to look like when they finished.

They spent a good portion of the morning searching the internet for contractors in the area before landing on a couple that had amazing reviews. Emily added them to the list, along with their phone numbers. By the time they finished breakfast and had a decent start on contractors they were going to look into, Anna knew they were already making great progress. Emily excused herself and went inside to get ready for the day. She cleaned up after breakfast and made sure that everything was put away. She was just finishing cleaning up the stove top attached to the side of the camper when Emily joined her outside once again.

"I made a few calls, and I found a man who is willing to come out and give us a quote. I also did a little more research on the guy before I gave him a call, and he seems to be well-liked in the area. The reviews said he's also fair when it comes to pricing."

Anna grinned. "That's amazing. I was expecting to split the phone calls, but I thought it was going to take most of the day to find a good contractor."

"It didn't take me long to get dressed, and I thought I could take care of it."

"That's good enough for me. Did he happen to say anything about what it is going to take to get the power turned back on?"

Emily nodded. "I did ask him, and he said the only thing we were going to need was a signature from him, and then they would turn the power back on."

9

Anna was excited by the fact that it wasn't going to take much to get started on the property. When they had discussed the topic the night before, she thought for sure it was going to be a long process and they would spend several nights in the camper. She was smiling and finishing the last of her clean-up duties when she saw a pickup truck pulling into the driveway with a ladder attached to the back. Whoever was driving was the man Emily had talked to on the phone, and she was surprised the guy was able to squeeze them in so soon after putting in a request for an estimate. It wasn't anything she was upset with since she was looking forward to having the ability to sleep inside. The sooner they were able to get started on the property, the sooner the job would be completed and they would have the ability to open the bed and breakfast.

The truck came to a stop halfway up the driveway, and Emily was already starting to walk in the man's direction. Anna was slowly following behind, anxious to see what the contractor would have to say when he got a good look around the mansion. It wasn't going to be a cheap adventure, but she was hoping the contractor would be willing to work with them, even if they were going to be able to get a loan for whatever they needed. When the door of the pickup truck opened and a teenage boy stepped out, Anna was stunned. She had expected to see a much older man, but it wasn't until she saw the other door open and an older man stepped out that she realized they were most likely a father-and-son crew. Smiling, knowing most small towns had family businesses, she approached the two men walking in their direction.

"My name is Peter Marshall, and this is my son, Justin. He works for me during the summer months. I believe I spoke to one of you on the phone just a little while ago."

Emily smiled and shook his hand. "You talked to me on the phone, and my name is Emily. This is my best friend, Anna. We were hoping to get an estimate on what it was going to take to get this place back up to specifications."

"We can certainly take a look at it. It's going to be a good thing for my business to add a place like this to my portfolio."

Anna smiled. "I don't know anything about

construction or what it's going to take to get this place up and running, but we did take a look around yesterday when we first got here. I'm pretty sure it's going to need a roof."

"From what I can tell from standing here, I'd say that's a good bet. It looks like you might have some leakage in that area up there," Peter said, pointing to the front right corner of the house where one of the towers stood.

"That's why we brought in the professionals. Emily said something about needing a signature from you in order to get the power turned back on."

"That's right. Once the power company knows there is actually going to be some work taking place here, they will be more than happy to turn it back on. I can't promise the kind of shape it's going to be in when we do, knowing it's probably been a while since it's been running."

Anna nodded. "I figured we were going to need some electrical components changed in the process, given how long ago this place was built."

"Many of these old houses end up rotting from the inside out, but I don't think you're going to have too much of an issue with the specifications. The little bit of knowledge I have about this place is that it was built with the right supplies."

"What do you mean?"

"Usually, buildings of this age were thrown together in a hurry, but the basic information I know about this place is that the family who built it had quite a bit of money. They certainly weren't known for cutting any corners when it came to their home."

Anna smiled. "I feel like that's a good thing, but I'm sure it's going to need plenty of work that the two of you are going to be able to take care of for us. I'm looking forward to finding out what you have to say about it."

"Let's go in and have a look around, then, shall we?"

The man hadn't even had a look around the property, and Anna had no idea what they were going to be charged for his services, but she was already leaning toward the idea they were going to be the contractors they hired to do the job. Peter seemed to be a good man, and his son looked as though he was built for hard labor. Between the two of them, she didn't think it would be hard for either of them to take care of the things that needed to be done. She also enjoyed the idea that they were local, and she would always choose local over corporate any chance she was given.

Peter was already looking at the front of the mansion, and by the look on his face, he was trying to get a better idea of what the outside would need. Anna was much more curious about the inside, even though she was well aware of what the exterior needed based on her basic knowledge of construction. It was going to need good paint, and if they were going to have to replace the windows, she was already trying to find a way to keep the basic structure of the house and the integrity of its history.

"This place is shrouded in a lot of lore," Justin said. "There are all kinds of stories about this place, but I'm sure you've already heard a few of them."

Peter laughed. "Let's not go scaring the customers off before we even get the job, son."

Anna chuckled. "You have nothing to worry about when it comes to stories that might shroud the property. We have every intention of rebuilding this place into something much better."

"I was just saying that there are plenty of old stories that go along with the mansion," Justin replied. "There's always been a lot of talk about this old house throughout town. I've heard those stories for as long as I can remember."

"I can't wait to hear all about it."

"You should know we actually write books for a living," Emily said. "Anna writes a lot about ghosts and true crime."

Anna could see a glow of excitement cross the young man's face, and although she was looking forward to hearing all the stories that came with the property, she wanted to know what Peter thought about the work that had to be done. As they started to head toward the front door of the mansion, Emily and Justin talked about the different stories they had both written in the past. It was nice to know the young man had some interest in what they did for a living, and she was glad the contractor had been able to arrive so fast. While she had been expecting everything to take more time, she was looking forward to getting started as soon as possible.

As Peter and Anna climbed the steps that led to the mansion's front porch, Anna started to get the same feeling she had earlier that morning. Someone was watching her, and she couldn't shake the notion, no matter how hard she tried. She started to turn her head to see if she could look around to find the culprit, but she changed her mind before she did. Her head was playing games with her, since she knew there was no one around earlier that morning, either. Simply shaking her head and pushing forward, she guided them up the stairs and directly to the front door.

10

Although Emily and Justin were behind them, talking about ghosts and writing, they had come to a stop several feet back. That left Anna and Peter on the porch alone, ready to enter the house and see what kind of work needed to be done. She was happy the young man and her friend had something in common to talk about so she could get the young man's father's opinion about how much work the mansion was going to need. By the time she actually opened the door, though, the man stopped before entering and smiled. The man had something to say, and she had no idea what it was going to be.

"I figure you should probably know I have been inside the house," Peter said. "I probably should have said that already, but I wanted to get to know you and your friend."

"Did they have you take a look around before the property was listed?"

"That's right. Although there might be some parts of the roof's structure that needs to be replaced, for the most part, it's in pretty good shape. It needs a few shingles, but I'm almost positive that the roof isn't going to need that much work."

"I'm glad you already have a good idea of what is going to need to be done."

Peter smiled. "I'm glad you said that. I wasn't sure how you were going to react to the fact that I had already looked into what the mansion would need. Although it might look rough, most of the work is going to be cosmetic."

"I could see that from the outside before we even walked in, but I thought there was a little water damage on the second floor when I got a good look around yesterday."

"From what I could tell when I looked at it a few weeks ago, it was simply some old damage that they had worked on years ago. I'm sure the majority of the electrical is going to need to be replaced. It's also going to need a new breaker box and an update to the wiring before the power is going to be able to be turned on."

"That sounds rather expensive. I thought we would be able to get the power switched on after we got the paperwork signed that you were going to do the work."

Peter nodded. "I'll have to turn the main breaker off so they can turn the power on to the house, but it shouldn't take that long to see some real progress on this place. I honestly can't wait to see this place up and running again."

There seemed to be some passion in the man's voice as he talked about the old mansion. Anna understood why they had brought in a contractor before raffling off the property, since it only made sense that the owners might not have wanted to do all the work themselves. Although she had no idea what kind of price tag would be on the necessary renovations, she was sure Emily's father would be able to get them the loan they would need to get the work started. Even as they stood right inside the doorway of the house, she caught herself glancing around the foyer and looking at the beauty it held within its walls. It was easy to see why it was possible for so many people to want to see the house in a working fashion again.

She had been sure from the original post on the website that it contained a lot of history, and although she wasn't quite sure about the background of the property, she was certain it was once a centerpiece for the community. The thought made her want to dig right into researching its history and what kind of secrets it would hold, knowing even if she didn't find anything, it could make for a good story for one of her books or blogs. As the two stood in the doorway, she thought about the price tag that would go along with the necessary work. Anna was already thinking about the income that would come from opening a bed and breakfast.

"I'm curious if the two of you have made any plans for what you want to do with this place."

Anna smiled. "Even before we knew we had won the raffle, we were talking about how nice a bed and breakfast location would be right here. It already has enough rooms to rent out on a regular basis."

Peter smiled. "That would definitely bring a lot of revenue to our little town. It's nice to know there are people in this world who have an eye for making old things beautiful once again."

"What do you mean?"

"Most of the time, people your age just want to tear things down and rebuild. I actually remember thinking that to myself when they talked about putting this place up for sale. I figured some millennials would come in and tear it down to make a coffee shop or something like that."

Anna shook her head. "We bought the tickets without even thinking we stood a chance of winning, but I'd rather see something good come from an old place like this than tear it down."

"It holds a lot of memories for the people of this town. You should also know the automatic gate box is going to need to be replaced as well. I should have said something earlier, but we got sidetracked talking about your plans."

"How much do those things cost?"

Peter chuckled. "You don't need to worry about that right this second. I'll go through the list of repairs I already have written down from the last time I was here and get you a quote. If anything, I'll work out a plan with you so that the two of you can make payments on the work I do."

When Anna heard Peter tell her they would be able to make a payment plan, she was stunned. She couldn't help but think about their trip to town the day before and how nice everyone seemed, let alone how nice everyone was the second time they had gone to town. She was starting to understand why so many people decided to settle in such obscure locations, and she wondered if it had something to do with the small-town vibe she had already started to feel. There was a lot she was going to have to learn about the area they were going to be living in, but she was glad that Emily had reached out to the man standing in front of her.

If anything they were planning to do was going to work out, they were going to have to have trustworthy people to deal with. Not only was Peter kind, but he also had a decent amount of knowledge when it came to the work that needed to be done on the old estate. It was a strange feeling to know not only did she own the property they were standing on, but they were about to renovate an area she honestly felt like she could call home. It wasn't until she turned back to the man standing next to her that she realized there had been an awkward silence between the two of them for several moments, and she chuckled nervously.

"I feel like I kinda got off in my own little world there, but I never expected to see so much kindness."

Peter smiled. "That's no big deal. I just assumed you were soaking in the idea of being the owner."

"I'm just shocked by how much potential this whole place has. I can see the beauty behind it all and what it might look like if we do things the right way. Is the rest of the town as kind as you are?"

"It's a small community, but a lot of people around here are going to be excited to see this old mansion redone. There are a lot of great memories here. Sometimes, this community can be a little harsh on newcomers, but for the most part, you'll find we tend to stick together and help one another when needed."

"What did you mean by there are a lot of good memories here?"

"I met my wife on a ghost hunt here at this house twenty-two years ago. We were just a couple of crazy young kids back then, but I can't wait to see this all open again. It's going to mean a lot to many people, and I'm excited to be the one working on it."

11

"It sounds like your wife is a very wonderful and adventurous woman. I can see why the two of you would be perfect for each other."

Peter sighed. "I think she would have liked you... I'm sorry. It's difficult for me to believe she's gone at times."

"I didn't mean to bring up any painful memories," Anna said.

"There's no way you could have known that my wife had passed away. She was a wonderful woman and would have loved to see what the two of you are going to do here."

"If you don't mind my asking, what happened to her?"

"She passed away from complications during

childbirth. It's hard to explain to someone who might not understand, but I can feel her presence with me almost daily. Don't get me wrong, I know she is gone and never coming back, but it feels like she is with me always."

Anna nodded. "It sounds like the two of you were very close, and that's probably why you feel like she is here. Even though you said you already know what the mansion is going to need, would you like to take another look around to make sure your list is complete?"

Peter nodded, but she could tell he was replaying the fond memories he shared with his wife from all those years before. As they entered the mansion and started to take a tour of the interior, Anna found herself wondering what the man's wife was like. He was easily one of the kindest people she had met in quite some time, and she was already looking forward to seeing him on a regular basis since she knew she was hiring him to do the work. They slowly made their way through the house, and he pointed out several items that were going to need to be repaired or replaced along the way. It was difficult to think that just a few days before, they had been planning on leaving the state of Louisiana, and now they were going to be living there full time.

It was a conversation the two of them also had, and Peter promised they were going to love the community. Just hearing the man say anything about the community sent a shiver up her spine. Anna hadn't been a part of a community in several years, and she wasn't even sure what it would mean. The one thing she was already clear about was the fact that it seemed like her family was growing. The man was obviously a good father. She could tell in the short amount of time she had spent with Justin, he was going to be just like his dad. It was easy to see that people raised with kind parents would also turn out the same way. If the rest of the community was just like the two people she had met, along with the mayor and financial advisor, she was going to love their new home.

Anna was practically leading the way, while Peter stopped in different spots and pointed out new items that could use touch-ups. From what she could tell and from what the man said, it did seem like most of the work was going to be cosmetic and paint. It sent a rush of relief through her mind, knowing she and Emily were going to be able to contribute in some ways. Anna looked forward to sitting down with Emily and discussing the color of paint they would be using, but she already knew she wasn't going to cover up any of the woodwork in the home. When the two of them reached the top of the staircase that led to the second floor, Peter stopped her and smiled.

"Justin was right about the fact that there are some stories about this place that you were probably going to hear eventually anyway. Do you know anything about the legend of Claymont Harrington?"

Anna shook her head. "Not really. I think when I was trying to do some research on the property before the raffle, I remember seeing the name. There's not much else I could tell you about him."

"The rumor around here is that Claymont Harrington had bars of gold he hoarded years ago. I'm sure there is some sort of back story that goes along with it, but I'm not exactly sure where the gold came from."

"Do you have any idea where I could find that information?"

Peter smiled and shrugged. "Not really. I'm sure there might be some old stories online that you can look up or check with the local library, but I've never dug into that part of its history."

"Are all the gold bars he hoarded supposedly somewhere in the house? I think I remember reading something about a hidden treasure here."

"That's right. The old story that has been shared around here throughout the years is that, at some point in his life, he decided that all of his children were evil to the core and they didn't deserve any of the money he had been collecting to hand down to them."

"So, I'm assuming he decided to leave them nothing."

Peter nodded. "They say the old man hid the gold

somewhere in the house, but it has never been found. There are many other ghost stories that go along with it, and there are some that aren't even close to the original story, but if you ask me, I doubt anything's here."

"What makes you say that?"

"This place was held by the Harrington heir all the way until they finally sold it to the county."

"What made them decide to do that?"

The man shrugged. "Honestly, I think that throughout the years of searching by the family and not coming up with anything, they just wanted to get as much money as they could out of place and not have to deal with the amount of time and renovations it would take to bring it to its former glory."

Anna smiled. "I guess it's a good thing that people like me and Emily own it now."

"I can tell that both of you are going to make good owners. I doubt there aren't too many people who would have come in here and decided to make something new out of it while keeping its history intact."

She grinned, knowing while most people would walk into the mansion and see a mess, she could see the beauty under all the things that needed to be fixed. Even without the back story to go with it, the mansion itself had a story of its own. Anna was hoping by the time everything was completed that she'd be able to tell its story to the world. There was something about the estate that was calling to her, and even though she was already there, she felt like it was trying to tell her something. The only thing for sure was she and Emily had plans to bring out the original beauty of the estate.

The two of them made their way through the second floor and entered each room as Peter continued to jot down notes in the small notebook he had kept in his pocket. He told her a few more stories about his wife, and she found herself wishing she could have met the woman. She sounded as kind and as joyful as the man she was walking through the mansion with, although it was easy to see that Peter missed the woman dearly. When the conversation died down and they were walking through the house, she started to think about the Harrington family. She wondered about the true story of the man who had supposedly hoarded gold bars and hit them in the mansion, but she was sure it was just something people started telling each other years before.

Anna knew that if there was any chance that there would be gold bars hidden in the house, there was no chance that the heir would have sold them to the county. If she had been part of the family, there was simply no chance she would have given up on the search. As the two of them started to make their way back down the staircase and toward the front door of the mansion, she couldn't stop thinking about the lore and the stories that seemed to surround the property. One way or another, she wanted to get as much information about its history as she could get her hands on, and when she finally found the answer she was looking for, she was already planning to write its story.

12

*A*nna was thinking about everything the man had told her and the amount of work that needed to be done on the estate when they reached the bottom of the staircase. She was glad they had found a contractor she felt like they could trust, and she was looking forward to getting started. As they began to make their way out of the front door of the mansion, she spotted Emily and Justin talking outside in the driveway. The two of them had hit it off just like she and Peter had. It became clear they were all going to get along without any problems, and it was nice to know everyone seemed to be on the same page when it came to their plans for the property.

"I was just thinking about how the power was running across the property, and I might be able to get ahold of the county and have the outdoor well pump and power to the garage turned on. If I remember correctly, I'm pretty sure the garage was hooked up separately."

"What does that mean?" Anna asked.

"It just means the garage was wired more recently and has a separate breaker box. We shouldn't have to be replaced," Peter replied.

"It'll be nice to have power for the camper and the van since we sort of live out of both of them."

"At least you won't have to worry too much about an extra power source or anything like that. I can't believe I almost forgot they weren't connected to the same breaker box."

"I assume it's been a little while since you've actually looked into everything here."

"Just a few weeks, but I think it's just because of the excitement I'm feeling about you and your friend starting to get work done here. I never imagined that anyone would buy this place and actually try to fix it up, but I'm happy to see that you have plans for its future that don't involve tearing it down."

Anna chuckled. "I just have an old soul. I can't tell you how thankful I am that you were willing to come out."

"I have to admit, the main reason I came so fast was because I wanted to find out what you had planned."

"Whatever your reasons, thank you."

Peter nodded, and the two of them headed toward the driveway after promising he would come back out later with the utility guy, along with the quote and payment plan for them to review. He climbed into his truck, and the two men pulled away. Anna found herself smiling as the two men drove off, and she knew the older man and his son were going to do a great job with all the work needed to be done on the mansion. Just knowing they were going to be getting some power to the camper soon was something she was grateful for, and although she wasn't exactly looking forward to seeing the price that would come with the work, she was happy that Peter was willing to set up a payment plan for them to get started.

Anna and Emily thanked him several times, and she appreciated everything he was willing to do to help them get everything going. When she had first woken up that morning, she thought about the long process and how much time would be spent just looking for a contractor, but as she waved to the man pulling out of her driveway, they had found the right person for the job. Not only was he willing to work with them to get the job paid, but he was also willing to go out of his way to make sure they had everything they needed.

Anna couldn't wait to work on her blog and let the world know about the kind of person she had met. Although she didn't have that many followers on her blog, she was hoping to at least get the information out in case anyone had planned on moving to the area. At the very least, she was ready to share all the information she had found about Harrington, Louisiana. It was only as she thought about where they were that she realized the name of the town was the same name that the owner of the property had been under. She was ready to start doing as much research as possible to find out more. Before she had the chance to think any further about her plans for the day, Emily moved closer and nudged her with her shoulder.

"Do you want to get another look at the inside and try to get in as much exploring as we can?"

Anna nodded. "Why do I feel like Justin told you something about the mansion that you want to look for? I feel like this has something to do with hidden treasure."

Emma chuckled. "If you know I want to look for something, then I'm going to assume that Peter told you something as well."

"He told me a story about hidden gold bars in the house. He said a man named Claymont Harrington decided that his children were evil and didn't deserve any of the money he had saved for them. Supposedly, he hid those gold bars in the house and they were never found."

"That lines up with everything Justin told me, except for one thing."

"What's that?"

Emily grinned. "Justin told me that the ghost of Claymont is hiding the treasure from the heirs. He said that his spirit drives the family away anytime they come to the estate."

"Yeah, Peter said there were several other stories that went along with the original, but I'm starting to wonder how many of those other stories are true."

"Something else he told me was that Claymont was hiding the treasure but that the heirs stopped by from time to time in order to try to find the treasure that's been hidden here for so long."

"I'm curious if the Harrington family is coming here to look for the treasure. I feel like if there was actually that much money hidden within the walls of the mansion, they would have torn it down by now."

Emily scoffed. "I thought about that as well, but I'm sure that if they had found the money, they would have wanted to keep the estate on top of it. Do you know how much a couple of gold bars go for these days?"

Anna shrugged. "Can't honestly say I have ever looked up the price before, but I might now that you have brought it up."

"We can do that later, but I want to get another look inside that house. I think it's possible that the whole story is true."

"As much as I would like it to be true, I doubt that much time has gone by and no one has been able to find it. It's not going to stop me from having a look around, but it's hard to believe they haven't been able to find a single clue as to where the treasure is hidden."

As much as she was enjoying the lore they were sharing with each other, Anna wondered how much truth was actually behind the stories. Peter had told her the Harrington family had sold the property to the county, which lined up with the fact that they had probably given up on their search. While the two of them made their way back into the house to get another look around, she couldn't stop thinking about the possibility of finding a hidden treasure within its walls. Even with the amount of love she had for the supernatural and ghost stories she had written, she wasn't sure how much of it she actually believed. There were several stories that were supposedly true, and she had used them as a base for another storyline in her books.

The more she thought about the situation they found themselves in and the story behind it all, she was already trying to think of how to incorporate it into her next book. Anna knew since her friend shared a lot of the same interests she had, the two of them might actually be able to come up with a perfect plot to cover all the stories at once. Before they started walking back toward the mansion's front door, Anna felt another chill run down her spine.

Although she was sure her mind was once again playing tricks on her, she found herself looking around to see if anyone was watching them. It was a feeling that continued on, even though she had yet to see anyone around.

13

"I think I might need you to pinch me," Anna muttered.

"Only if you do the same for me. I am happy it is not just in my head. This place is unreal, right?"

Anna nodded, looking over the ornate details that the original craftsman had put into not only the public parts of the house but the private as well. It was unreal to see such beauty, but it was also a little heartbreaking to know it had sat in disrepair for so long. She couldn't fathom ever letting a thing of such beauty go to waste. It was baffling to her that anyone would even consider letting the home reach a state of such heartbreaking deterioration.

"Wouldn't it be wild if we found the treasure?" Emily asked.

"I wouldn't get your hopes up. This place has been gone over with a fine toothcomb dozens of times by people far more equipped to find a legendary treasure than us. But I love your enthusiasm. Plus, isn't winning the auction treasure enough?"

Her friend groaned and rolled her eyes. "Sure, but I didn't think when you found a treasure that it was supposed to cost you money…"

"Are you having second thoughts?"

"Not on your life!" Emily blurted out. "You aren't going to get rid of me that easily. I am in this for the long haul."

"Good because, quite frankly, I don't think I could do this without you. Taking on this project is…huge, to say the least."

"Don't worry, I'm not going anywhere. I can't wait to find all the secrets this place is hiding."

"You and me both," Anna said.

It was both a thrilling and terrifying task they were undertaking. All around her, though, the ornate details of the property reminded her of what a wonderful retreat it could make for other writers and artists like themselves. That alone gave her enough determination to want to see the house restored to what it once was. Even the fireplace, with its single large slat of stone, had carvings that would take skilled masters a decade to complete. She couldn't fathom the anger that Claymont Harrington had to be harboring to leave it all behind, knowing it would crumble into the ground.

"So, do you think there is any truth to the stories?" Emily asked.

Anna shrugged. "They say most legends and ghost stories are rooted in some sort of truth. Do I think the old man buried actual treasure here? No. But I definitely think he lived here and disliked his own offspring enough to leave them nothing."

"What makes you think that?"

"From what little we have learned so far about him, all of this took place right around the same time as the stock market crash and the Great Depression. I think he lost everything except the land and house. Then? He died a bitter old man who refused to admit he had lost everything."

"Wow, you paint a far more depressing picture than the haunted house and jaded family that I've read about online…"

Anna grinned at her friend. They had only been able to travel the country because of their work as true crime storytellers and fiction writers. It was in their blood that they wanted to learn the truth, whether it was ghosts, goblins, or good old-fashioned murder. The Harrington estate was the perfect piece of property for the friends. She was beyond excited to start making it their home. It was easy to understand why Emily was intrigued by the lore surrounding the estate. The idea of it being haunted and the home to a hidden treasure was far more intriguing.

No matter what, though, they would uncover the

truth. She could already see the lucrative end of things. Though it was the intriguing mystery that had originally piqued their interest, now it had become a personal goal of hers to see where the story led. She found it hard to believe that Claymont Harrington would leave behind a fortune without knowing if it would ever be found. Yet the lore was going to draw in a huge crowd. Given most businesses lost money within the first few years of operating, they would need all the media buzz they could get for their grand opening whenever that time came.

"I don't even know where we're supposed to start," Emily muttered.

"That makes two of us. We will figure it out. Someone around here has to know something about this place, right?"

"Speaking of which, I was doing some digging for businesses in the area that we might be able to partner with to save some money on restorations, and I stumbled across an antique shop."

Anna chuckled and shook her head. "Leave it to you to start shopping before we even have the lights on."

Emily gave her a grin and rolled her eyes. "Actually, it was the owner who intrigued me. Apparently, she is the local historian and would be the person to talk to about this place and its stories. Of course, it doesn't hurt that she happens to own an antique store as well. God knows we are going to need a few old pieces to make this place feel authentic…"

"See now, if you had stopped at the local historian, we would be golden."

The pair both chuckled. Emily knew Anna was only joking around with her. One of the things Anna loved about their friendship was how similarly their beliefs, goals, and financial plans lined up with each other. Neither of them liked to spend money if it wasn't necessary, though Emily had a fondness for unique and rare antiques. It was a passion that would definitely help see them through the next couple of weeks as they tried to outfit the estate with era-appropriate furniture and décor. She had every intention of letting Emily take the wheel when it came to the pieces they picked and what went on the walls.

As much as Anna enjoyed the final outcomes, she was not a fan of the assembly process. As far as she was concerned, Emily could do whatever she wanted with the various spaces, and Anna knew beyond a shadow of a doubt that the end result would be stunning. Looking around yet another dilapidated and depressing room, Anna shook her head and let out a heavy sigh. There was no doubt they had their work cut out for them. If they could keep the project funded, there was a slim chance they might be able to open in October for all the ghost and ghoul enthusiasts.

"I already see the wheels turning in your head,"

Emily said. "Don't start stressing out about everything. This house only cost two hundred dollars. We will make it work, got it?"

Anna nodded. "Yeah, I got it. I am happy you bought those tickets. This is the start of something amazing, and I know it. I guess it is all just a little overwhelming at the same time."

"Trust me, I understand. I know we always have my father to fall back on, but neither of us wants to see that happen."

"I couldn't agree more. Do you think we will be able to open by October?"

"Who knows? I think as determined as we both are to do this on our own, it's going to take a lot of hard work… But it's you and me we are talking about here. We can do anything we put our minds to."

Anna smiled. "I couldn't agree more."

"Plus, if nothing else, we can always just light a match, watch it burn, and go back out on the road. We were happy before this place, and I know we will be happy long after it's gone."

"Maybe we should at least try to restore it before you start a fire," Anna said.

"Fine, have it your way. Just know I am ready with the roasting sticks and marshmallows whenever you say the word. This place is pretty wonderful, but it's not worth the headache if it starts driving a wedge between us." Emily gave her a playful wink.

"I think we have a pretty good idea of everything

that needs to be done here. What do you say we go get the van set up over by the garage?" Anna asked.

Emily nodded, and the pair slowly made their way back through the house to the main doors. For a split second, Anna could have sworn she felt eyes upon her, but as she glanced back around the dilapidated structure, she saw nothing. As strange as it was, it wasn't the first time she had felt the eerie sensation since their arrival at the property. Though she wanted to believe there was no such thing as ghosts, she couldn't shake the nagging feeling that something was trying to get her attention.

14

The pair headed for the van parked with the small camper attached. Veering off, Anna made her way to the garage to start working and open the doors while Emily climbed behind the wheel of their home. It took all of her muscles to tug open the massive antique garage doors. She nearly lost her grip when the cloud of dust finally died down, revealing a hidden gem that made Anna's heart race. Sitting beneath a thick layer of the same dust that assaulted her was a 1967 Chevy Impala. The black body of the beast appeared to be in mint condition.

At that moment, Anna forgot all about helping Emily navigate the van and camper. Behind her, she heard the van shut off and the door open but didn't turn around. Instead, she moved forward, running her fingers along the beautiful classic muscle car. When she peered through the clouded driver's side window, her racing heart quickened once more at the sight of the keys dangling from the ignition. Though she half expected to pop the trunk and find it full of salt guns, holy water, and pentagrams, Anna was drawn to the seat behind the wheel. The car called to her, begging her to slip inside. It was magnificent.

Emily gave a low whistle just as Anna opened the driver's door, her body tingling with excitement as she smiled at her friend. One of the many shared appreciations they had was that of classic cars. Though Emily had owned a few over the years, courtesy of her father, the Impala was Anna's first real vehicle. She had to fight back tears at the sight of it.

"Oh damn, she sure is a beauty…" Emily said. "Pop the hood for me?"

Anna didn't hesitate to open the door and climb behind the wheel, pulling the lever for the hood latch as she ran her hands across the leather seats. It felt like a dream. The shock and joy of winning the estate lottery paled in comparison to finding the car. With the house, it was going to take a ton of money and time to bring it back to life, but the sleek, black muscle car might be easily restored. It would be a fun side project for them. Anna could hear Emily fiddling around under the hood.

"I have to tell you, this thing is clean for its age. It's damn lucky it was stored inside. I've seen sixty-sevens covered in rust because the owners didn't take care of them," Emily said.

"It's just so strange that someone would leave it here without giving a shit about it. It breaks my heart to think of the love it took for someone to care for it in its early days, only to be discarded again. Who would do that?"

"Trust me, I've seen it all over the years. People forget about the car or bike that their great-grandfather's second cousin had before passing away. They're forgotten relics of the past, and most people just don't care about them."

"What a shame," Emily muttered. "Wait till you see the interior of this lady. I don't see a single sign of wear and tear. It's like someone drove it right off the line and parked it."

"Yeah, that's what I'm getting under the hood, too. I can see that it's been messed with a little, but nothing major. I'm in shock that it's in here. Makes me wonder what else we are going to find."

Anna chuckled. "I can almost hear the wheels turning in your head. There is no hidden treasure or lost famous painting in that place. I can guarantee you that."

"Hey now, don't be crushing a girl's dreams like that. Look at this thing. It *is* the treasure of this estate."

"I can't argue with that," Anna muttered.

She had never seen anything quite like the car in person, and knowing it was now hers only elated her more. Luck had never been on Anna's side, at least not until she had met Emily. With Emily, the woman's positivity had raised Anna to a new level. She didn't want to think about how different things would have been had their paths never crossed. Turning her attention back to the Impala, Anna could almost hear the engine rumbling in her mind. When it had a wash and a little TLC, it would be a thing of a dreams without question.

As she daydreamed about driving the beast, Anna listened to her friend tinkering around under the hood. Twice, she disappeared into the back of the garage, though Anna couldn't see what she'd brought back with her because of the hood. While she had a vast appreciation for the beautiful craftsmanship of classic muscle cars, Anna knew almost nothing about the mechanics. That was where her best friend shined. She couldn't count the number of times Emily's knowledge had saved them from a massive tow or technician bill. The hood came back down, and Anna jumped into the passenger seat.

"Well?" Emily said.

"Well, what?"

"Give it a go!"

"What? No way, man. This thing has been sitting here for at least twenty years. There is no way it's going to start," Anna said.

Emily shrugged. "You won't know until you try. Plus, it looks like someone has been tinkering under the hood fairly recently, and there is a fresh gas can.

I'd say they tried to get it running before the auction but couldn't and gave up."

"So, what makes you think it's going to start for me now?"

Her friend grinned. "One of the spark plugs was shot. It looks like they tried to replace them but didn't do it right. I found a few spares on the shelf by the door, and there is a gas can over there, too. The fuel is fresh, so this baby might just fire up for you."

She took a deep breath, her hand moving to the key. Wrapping her fingers around the cool metal, Anna couldn't help but close her eyes and say a silent prayer as her hand started to rotate. Suddenly, the ancient beast grumbled to life, barely missing a beat as the horses roared. The vibrations of the powerful engine moved through her body, bringing with it a deep appreciation for the quality of the engineers. They had created a dream car when it came to the Impala. Looking at Emily, Anna got the nod of approval as she slipped it into gear and then backed slowly out of the garage.

"I can't believe this," Anna stammered. "This beast is worth more than the house at this point."

Emily laughed. "Let's get the dust off her and take her for a spin. How does that sound? There are three bays in the garage, so we've got plenty of space to park the van and camper."

"I love it."

She parked the Impala and prayed once more

before shutting it off. If it didn't start for them again, Anna knew she'd be kicking herself for pulling it out. Thankfully, there was a slight slope to the driveway, making it easier to push the muscle car back into the garage if it came down. While Anna worked on getting the camper and van parked, thanks in part to the cameras they had on the outside of both, Emily found a handful of shop rags and started wiping down the car. It didn't take long before the garage was once more buttoned up and the car was shining. Standing back to admire her work, Anna shook her head as Emily approached.

"I didn't find a single spot of rust anywhere on the body. Do you know how rare that is for something this old?" Anna asked.

"I'm telling you, girl, this thing is in pristine shape. I don't know why anyone would leave it behind…"

They were both baffled by it as they climbed back into the vehicle. She adjusted the mirrors with Emily's help before turning the car on once more. With the motor rumbling, Anna turned on the radio for the first time as a classic playing in the cassette deck filled the silence. She couldn't stop herself from immediately singing along to the Kiss song while Emily rocked along next to her. Slipping the shifter into gear, they slowly rolled down the driveway and onto the road. As they went, Anna tapped the brakes several times to make sure everything was in working order. It was amazing to her that the car had started, let alone that she could drive it down the road.

Not one to look a gift horse in the mouth, Anna turned up the radio and cranked the window down. Emily did the same, now singing at the top of her lungs the same as Anna. With a warm summer breeze moving through the car, she could feel all her worries and trepidations about the estate starting to fade away. For the first time in her life, Anna felt like she was free.

15

"Never in my life did I think you'd be driving this bad boy off the property so fast," Emily said.

"You aren't kidding! She's running like a dream, though. It's about as smooth as you could want for a car sitting in a garage for years. How'd the tires look?"

"Cherry, which makes no sense. The whole thing is just downright baffling, if you ask me."

"Chalk it up to another mystery of the Harrington house. Something tells me we are going to learn a lot more about that property before it's all said and done," Anna said.

"I'm going to start a list of what we need for the van and for the house. I think we should pull into the first station we see. The gas wasn't bad, but that doesn't mean I trust it, either," Emily said.

"You've got it."

They continued to cruise through the countryside and winding road that would eventually lead them into town. It wasn't long before a two-pump station came into view between the waves of forest that lined the road. She steered the Impala up to one of the empty pumps and killed the engine. At the same time, Emily was finishing their list. Anna didn't need to know what her friend was adding. They'd been traveling together for so long that she would bet money on knowing every item on the list. The only variable that ever changed was the alcohol, depending on where they were and if there were any good wineries in the vicinity.

Making their way into the small station, an elderly man watched them intently from behind the counter. The pair perused the aisles until they managed to find a few drinks for the road. Though she didn't normally approve of them, Anna knew she needed the potent energy drink she was setting on the counter next to Emily's soda. Jerking her head toward the car outside, she asked for twenty in fuel as she pulled cash from her wallet.

"You've sure got yourselves a 'beaut out there," he said.

She grinned. "Don't I know it? Run's like a champ, too."

"I ain't seen that car in damn near forty years now, but I'd know the license plate anywhere."

Anna paused. "Wait, you know the car?"

He nodded. "Sure do, belonged to the Harrington family. If memory serves, the old man Claymont bought it himself. Hell, I thought they'd sold it off, though, along with all the other valuables years ago."

"No, we found it in the garage. We just bought the place," she muttered. "You said Claymont Harrington bought it? Was he from the area? Does he have family here?"

"Hell, you can't spit without hittin' a relative of the Harrington family around here. That bloodline goes back really far. Us folks joke that one way or another, we're all related."

"Got it," Anna said.

"All the same, I'm mighty glad to see that someone is out driving the old girl around. Claymont would be tickled pink that she was hitting the road."

"Well, we are happy she's on the road, too."

After thanking the man and paying for the gas and drinks, she headed back out to the car, where Emily was wrapping up with the gas. Climbing into the passenger seat, Anna gave her best friend a wink as she tossed her the keys. The look of pure joy in Emily's expression made Anna burst into laughter. She was like a kid in a candy store all over again. It was heartwarming to see. Anna loved being able to share the wonderful new treasure with her best friend. In the back of her mind, the lingering knowledge that they might not get to keep the car continued to poke at her. It would break Emily's heart, but at least they could enjoy it for a little while.

"You look like someone just stole your last cookie. Penny, for your thoughts?" Emily said.

Anna grinned. "Sorry, I was just thinking about all the work that needs to be done on the house. I don't know how we are going to afford it."

"Don't worry. The contractor said he'd work with us on payments, and my father could always give us a little loan. With the new material we'll be able to post online, I bet our numbers will double. You'd be surprised how much people love a good DIY project."

"I hope you are right, but maybe we should talk about putting some feelers out on the Impala…"

Emily's gaze whipped away from the road to Anna. In the look, she saw the pure horror at the suggestion to sell the Impala. It wasn't something she wanted to do by any means, but the money would provide them with a safety net they were desperately lacking. It was true they could always borrow from Emily's father, but neither of them wanted to do that.

"Have you lost your ever-loving mind? Why would you even say something like that?" Emily bellowed.

"Take it easy now. I'm not saying it's going to happen, but—"

"You can't, Anna. This thing is a piece of the estate's history. It's a lynchpin in the lore of the whole mansion. Think about the cult following something like her might attract."

"Again, it was just an idea...

"Well, it's not a very good one. Hell, that's right up there with leaving it sitting in the garage. A car like this deserves to be loved, to be driven and feel the open road, not tucked away in some garage or museum for the rest of its life."

Anna rolled her eyes. "You know it doesn't actually have feelings, right? It doesn't care where it's at or who is driving it...it's just metal and bolts."

Suddenly, the car lurched forward, chugging at the gas in the engine. The unexpected movement sent Anna flying toward the dash. She barely kept herself from smacking her head. Given how things had been up to that point, it was incredibly unnerving. For a split second, she wondered if she'd been wrong and if the vehicle had a mind of its own. The very notion was only slightly out of her realm of comfort. Given Anna's belief in just about everything supernatural, a Christine-style car wasn't all that far-fetched. Her eyes darted to Emily, who looked more amused than shaken.

"You sure about that?" Emily asked. "Doesn't sound like the old girl liked that too much..."

She sighed. "Fine. I'm sorry. You're more than just a hunk of metal."

Once more, the Impala started running as it had been for the majority of their drive. Though she was skeptical it was anything more than the old gas cycling through the motor, Anna knew better than to tempt fate for a second time. She wanted to believe the mansion would make enough money to keep them afloat, but it didn't seem likely. Emily, on the other hand, loved believing in the impossible. She could remember the first time her best friend had mentioned her belief in the paranormal. It was like finding a kindred spirit, a one-in-a-million occurrence, that Anna thanked God for every single day. They were soulmates, though not in the romantic sense.

That single conversation had sparked a lifetime of adventure with a woman Anna adored. There was no question that the universe held more than met the naked eye, but the debate on where that line was drawn could change from day to day depending on what Anna witnessed firsthand. She wasn't about to claim that the car wasn't possessed by the long-dead Claymont Harrington. After all, stranger things had happened. Chuckling, she shook her head and thought about the mansion they now owned that had only cost them a few hundred dollars in entry fees. That alone made her a believer in the notion that, quite literally, anything was possible.

"All I'm saying is that I've seen this year and model going for upwards of one-hundred-thousand dollars in pristine condition. Even a third of that amount would get the ball rolling on the repairs—"

"You've lost your damn mind. I swear if you try to sell this car, I will have you committed to an insane asylum, do you hear me? We'll find a way to get the repairs made without selling our souls in the process."

Anna wanted to point out to her friend that it was just a car, but it would only make things worse. Instead, she gazed out at the beautiful landscape, hoping that Emily was right and they wouldn't have to put the car on the auction block. It was the last thing she wanted to do, but she knew the moment they started work on the estate, they'd need something more lucrative than their blogging. Until that time came, she would let her friend keep living the dream.

16

Driving through the picturesque community, she was by how classic it all seemed. Whoever kept watch over the layout and vibe of the main street was obviously going for a vintage appeal. It was well worth it, given how popular the area seemed to be with tourists. That small glimpse into the community warmed her heart. Anna wanted to be a part of it all and bring in more revenue for the small businesses by opening the bed and breakfast. All good things take time. She wasn't going to start rushing the process, no matter how excited they became.

In her mind, Anna couldn't help but wonder how much faster they could get the business open with a little financial help from selling the car. Emily wouldn't be on her side in the argument for letting it go. Over time, Anna planned on slowly working her friend down until she found the reason. Something told her that after the first few thousand, they had to pull from savings, and Emily would be singing a different tune. Glancing back at the car as they headed for the small storefront, she shook her head.

"I can see what you're thinking. You should forget about it right now 'cause I'm not going to budge," Emily said. "I'd take out a loan from my father before we sell that baby."

She chuckled and rolled her eyes. "It's weird. You know what people are thinking, right?"

Emily shrugged. "I like it. It's like a little superpower. Not all of us can cast spells with our writing alone."

"Is that what it is? Not hard work and years of building a following?"

"Nope. Magic," Emily said.

She laughed at her friend's dramatic hand flourishes as she headed into the storefront. Right away, Anna nearly plowed into Emily's back. Her friend had stopped right inside the door. It didn't take long for Anna to see why. Behind the counter was a gorgeous woman who appeared in her early twenties. Her sandy-blond hair draped over one shoulder and onto the glass display case as she hunched over a painting with a pair of tweezers. It was easy to see that the woman was engrossed in the restoration project. Despite a bell overhead alerting her to the door opening, she barely moved.

"Be right with you," the woman muttered.

"My God," Emily whispered. "I think I'm in love, Anna."

Anna grinned and moved past her friend. "You don't know a thing about her. I think you're drooling. Do I need to make you wait in the car?"

"There isn't enough manpower in the world to get me to leave this place now…"

Once more, she had to fight back laughter. Emily had dated different women on and off over the years, but it was rare for her to find anyone she liked enough to see them more than a handful of times. There had been times when she thought that her friend might want to stick around in one town or another for a girl, but in the end, they always pulled away, leaving a trail of broken hearts behind them. As Anna turned her attention back to the shop and the wonderful assortment of collectibles and trinkets, she forgot all about Emily and her pursuit of the shopkeeper.

For the first time in as long as she could remember, Anna felt herself wishing their financial situation was a little better. Every piece the store had decorating the walls and shelves was downright exquisite. The woman took great pride not only in her work but in the pieces she displayed. Anna could have easily spent hours looking through the different paintings, décor, and furnishings. She never wanted to leave. After some time wandering through the shop on her own, Anna heard Emily calling out for her from the front. When she managed to find her way back to the counter, it came as no shock that Emily was grinning from ear to ear.

The woman was obviously just as intrigued by Emily as her friend was with the locals. Given their plans to put down roots in the area, all Anna could do was hope that Emily wouldn't work her way through town, breaking hearts and causing havoc where they planned to live. It was a conversation best had for when the pair were back at the van. She didn't want to call her friend out for her playgirl behavior in front of the stranger. Smiling as Emily introduced her to the shopkeeper, Anna turned her attention back to the matters at hand.

"It's a pleasure to meet you, Anna. I'm Lori Young. I own this little place here," she said.

"Well, it's downright magnificent if you ask me. You've got a beautiful collection here," Anna said.

"Thank you. Emily tells me that you two are the new owners of the Harrington estate? I have to tell you, as the local historian, I am just tickled pink to see something happening with that place. I thought for sure it was going to be torn down sooner or later. Are the rumors true that you plan on opening a business?"

"That's the plan. Hopefully, it goes off without too many problems. I know anything is possible with a project of that size," Anna said.

"Well, in either case, I think it's just about the

neatest place I've ever seen...not that I've seen much of it at all, just from the outside when I'm out that way."

"So, you've never seen the inside of it?" Emily asked.

Lori shook her head. Right away, Anna knew where her friend was going with the question, but she wasn't about to step on Emily's toes. For the first time, she noticed a sparkle in her friend's gaze that wasn't normally there. At that moment, she knew the small business owner was different from the women who Emily had courted in the past. Anna was beyond happy for her friend. If anyone deserved a happy ending, it was Emily.

"Only on the internet and in my dreams," Lori said. "I tried to get inside to do an article for our little local paper but was pretty much stonewalled. It's a shame, too. I'd have loved to bring attention to it years ago."

"Well, it might be a little late, but I am glad you got shut down. At least this way, I got to meet you," Emily said.

The woman blushed, her dark eyes glistening with emotions as she smiled at Emily. Anna had all the confirmation she needed. The pair were obviously smitten with each other. Anna supported it as long as Emily was careful. They couldn't afford any ill will from the locals, and a relationship soured would certainly not do them any favors. As the pair turned their attention and the conversation to their shared interest, Anna knew she was going to have to drag Emily out of there if they hoped to get anything done on the house. It was wonderful to see Emily so happy. She cleared her throat, and they both turned to look at her.

"I hate to be the one to break up the party, but we've got the contractor coming out in a little bit to give us an estimate. We should be heading back," Anna said.

Emily sighed. "Yeah, I suppose you are right. I guess we should do some adulting today."

"I'm so sorry. I didn't realize I was keeping you guys from getting work done. Please feel free to stop in anytime or give me a call if there is anything I can help you with. I'm just so excited to know someone is going to be taking care of that place after all this time."

"Well, we could certainly use some help decorating the place. Maybe you should come up and see it, you know…to give you an idea of what we want to do with the old girl," Emily said.

The woman's eyes lit up. "Really? Oh my gosh, that would be a dream come true. I've been dying to see inside. I mean, it's amazing just from the road but up close…" Lori gave a low whistle as Emily continued to grin.

"Then why don't you come up a little later on this

afternoon? Say around six? I could probably even whip us up some dinner," Emily said.

"How about I bring Chinese instead? That way, you don't have to fuss with it. There is a great place in the next town over."

"It's a date then," Emily said.

Once more, Lori blushed as Anna made her way to the door. Thankfully, Emily soon followed her, and Anna didn't have to drag her out of the shop like a toddler. On the street, she let the warm sunlight wash over her as Emily moved to her side, smiling like a man who had just seen heaven for the first time.

17

"A date, huh?" Anna said.

Emily gave her a wink. "Well, she didn't correct me, so that's something, right?"

Anna chucked once more. She adored her friend for being so hopeful. It did seem as though the woman was just as interested in Emily as her friend was in Lori. Plus, it was wonderful knowing they would have a local on their side as long as Emily could play nice. She wanted to believe it was a match made in heaven, but a rough life had jaded her some. It wasn't as though she could suddenly start trusting people, not when she'd spent most of her life trying to survive without the outside world screwing her in some way or another.

"You look like the cat who got the canary," Anna said. "I hope you plan on acting with your head and no other body parts."

"Ha! Oh, you've got nothing to worry about. That one is special. I could tell right away. I just hope she's interested."

"Are you kidding me? She was giving off vibes so strong I'm surprised it didn't register as an earthquake. You know, I think I finally understand what they mean about love being blind now. She was definitely into you."

"Good," Emily said. "That feeling is definitely mutual. Man, I hope she comes tonight…"

"Don't worry, she'll be there. We won't be much longer, though, if we don't get back to meeting the contractor. You ready to hit the road?" she asked.

Before they could climb back into the Impala, the door behind them opened, and Lori came bursting out onto the street. She looked a little embarrassed. Her eyes had moved from Emily to the car sitting in front of her shop. The woman's cheeks flushed red as her jaw dropped for a split second in shock. They both stood, baffled and waiting for an explanation.

"Oh my God, is that your car?" Lori stammered. "Do you know who that belonged to? I didn't see what you pulled up in until now…holy cow."

"Wait, you know the car?" Emily asked.

She nodded, moving toward it with an appreciation Anna had seen not long before in her friend's own eyes. Once more, she was convinced that Emily had found a partner after her own heart. Anna had to keep from grinning as Lori looked over the preserved classic.

"This car was Claymont Harrington's. There are so many stories about it, but never in my life did I think I would be seeing it up close and in person. Jeez, I thought it was long gone decades ago…"

"What do you know about it?" Anna asked. "We are interested in knowing just about anything we can about the estate and the family."

"Oh man, you came to the right shop then. They say Claymont Harrington's ghost haunts the car and that he's not tied to the house but the sixty-seven instead. Hell, they went over this thing with a fine-toothed comb, looking for his millions after he died."

"I take it they never found anything?" Anna asked.

Lori shook her head. "Nope, no fortune, except the priceless treasure you see in front of you. Wow. I can't believe it's running and here. What are you going to do with it?"

Anna frowned. "We haven't decided—"

"We're keeping it. It deserves to be loved, you know?" Emily said.

She glared at her friend for a split second but didn't want Lori to see them at odds.

"That's awesome," Lori said.

"Maybe you and I can go for a cruise down the back roads one of these nights soon," Emily said.

Lori blushed. "Oh, I'd like that a lot."

"All right, you two, we need to get going," Anna

said. "I can guarantee that your readers will want to hear about this car and the lore, Emily. We should get back to the manor."

"Yeah, yeah, I know you're right, and those followers are going to help pay for the renovations," Emily said.

"So, you're a writer?" Lori asked.

Emily nodded. "We both are, actually, with an affection for hauntings and the paranormal. Finding the Harrington estate and winning that auction was destiny."

Anna knew that if she didn't step in once more, she'd find herself the third wheel on a spontaneous afternoon date for the pair, and they didn't have time for that. Before long, she would just leave Emily behind to find her own ride home while she went and met with the contractor. Clearing her throat, she caught her friend's eye and silently reminded her they needed to get going. Emily nodded and wrapped things up with Lori. Moments later, the shopkeeper was once more inside her little oasis, and they were reaching for the car's doors again. Suddenly, her friend paused, looking past Anna at something else.

"Uh oh," Emily muttered.

She cocked her head. "What?"

"Excuse me!" came a familiar voice.

She spun around to see Nancy Thomas walking briskly in their direction, waving her hand in an angry manner as she went. The woman was heading for them, giving little care to the scene her shouting and waving were causing as people came and went from the shops on the main road through the community. Never one to like attention, Anna flushed immediately and glanced around. It had been a mistake she regretted right away. A handful of people had now stopped to see what was happening, noticing the car and talking amongst themselves.

Relief surged through her when Emily moved around from the other side of the car to stand next to her. Though she was capable of handling the woman on her own, it wasn't something Anna enjoyed, unlike Emily. Her friend was always looking for a way to poke the bear, no matter who it was. Generally, all Anna had to do was stand back and occasionally remind Emily she didn't look good in orange jumpsuits. The flush of the woman's cheeks from moving at a brisk pace amused her a little, but she kept the smirk off her lips, which was more than Emily had managed to do.

"How on *earth* did you get that piece of junk down onto the main road? I hope you don't plan on leaving it there because I will have it towed. As a matter of fact, who towed it here to begin with, huh? We've got an image to uphold," Nancy growled.

"Whoa, now, take it easy there," Emily said. "We drove it down here, no tow truck needed, and she's most certainly not a piece of junk, either. Hell, she purrs like the day she first rolled off the assembly line fifty-seven years ago."

"Well, that's just a pile of lies, and I know it to be true. A good half-dozen mechanics tried to get that pile of scrap out of the garage and couldn't do it," Nancy said.

Emily shrugged. "I guess she didn't like them like she does us."

Nancy glared at her. The woman wasn't happy about the village's lost financial gain. Though Anna could applaud how dedicated she was to the community, she didn't appreciate the hostile manner in which they were being approached. There were so many other ways that Nancy could have spoken to them, but the woman obviously enjoyed the position of authority she had within the confines of the area. It didn't give her the right to be hostile, though, not when Emily and Anna had done nothing wrong.

"Fine, have it your way, but you aren't making any friends acting like an entitled brat," Nancy growled. "I see you don't have tags on the vehicle. Get them, or the next time, I'll have you towed and tossed in jail for good measure."

Emily snorted. "Whoa, take it easy, lady—"

"Don't you speak to me in that tone," Nancy snapped.

Anna knew she had to step in. Grabbing hold of her friend's arm, she promised Nancy they'd get tags on the car immediately and dragged Emily to the driver's side of the car. As she shoved the -cussing woman behind the wheel, Anna slammed the door and gave Nancy one last wave before jumping into the passenger seat. Her friend glared at her but said nothing as she turned the key and slipped the muscle car into reverse. If looks could kill, Nancy would have dropped dead on the sidewalk as Emily peeled away from the main drag.

So far, they weren't making many friends in the area, and Anna knew that could prove fatal for a new business. Somehow, they had to find a way to keep the peace and make things work with Nancy, no matter how much she seemed to dislike the two. As the country took over the view, Anna let her worries and fears slip away. They had found a place to call home, and no one could take that joy away from them, not even the bitter woman.

18

"What in the hell was her problem?" Emily stammered.

She shook her head. "The hell if I know. I never thought that would be the reaction we got tough. Did you see how people were staring at us?"

"Let them," Emily growled. "I've had backwoods hicks judging me since I first slid my fine stiletto-wearing ass out of the closet."

Anna chuckles. "I love you for that. Your thick hide gives me strength. I just wish it wasn't needed at all, especially here, where we'll be putting down roots."

"Yeah, well, the locals are going to figure out really quickly that if they want a show, I'll give them one. Here we are busting ass to make the estate something great and they want to treat us like lepers."

"It's going to take time. We'll bring them around

eventually. You're far too charming not to befriend a few of them. You like Lori, right? I bet we'll find our people before long," Anna said.

She desperately wanted to believe her own words, but there was a lingering doubt in her mind that there would ever be an acceptance. Whatever the town's financial advisor thought about them was destined to trickle down into the rest of the community. She hated that it was happening at all but knew all good things took time. They could find a way to navigate the politics of the community, just as they had done in the past. As the estate once more came into view, she let her worries slip away. Though there was a slightly daunting and foreboding atmosphere about it, Anna refused to let it suck her in.

"All right, I'm going to get the van and camper moved into place so we can hook it up in the garage and start breaking down this old girl. I am positive with a tune-up and new plugs that she's going to purr even more than she already does," Emily said.

"Good, I'll start getting our before pictures for the website," Anna replied.

"Okay, just be careful poking around in there. We don't need a hospital bill for a round of rabies or tetanus shots..."

"You're preaching to the choir, sister. Have you seen our views since posting about the estate, though? People are definitely hooked on the saga. I want to make sure we've got enough images to keep them intrigued," she said.

As her friend brought the car to a stop outside the garage and they both climbed out, she gazed at the home that now belonged to her. It was so strange to think she was a homeowner, even if it was nearly in ruins. Someday, it would be magnificent, but keeping that dream alive required money, and that came from posting material that people wanted to read and follow. It had taken them years to make money in the industry, and now, it would finally be paying off. Twenty minutes after making it back to their little oasis, she was popping her battery into the camera and climbing the front steps of the estate.

Time ceased to have all meaning as she moved through the house with her camera at the ready. Everywhere she looked was another photo opportunity that Anna couldn't pass up. They had stumbled on a treasure trove of collectibles that would look great once they had a little love and attention. Hopefully, Emily and Lori will continue to get along. Anna was positive that the woman would be a great addition to their renovation and restoration team if Emily could keep from breaking her heart. Room by room, she snapped photos of the dust-covered curtains and crumbling bricks that needed repair.

Instead of focusing on the sole project of future posts, she snapped a handful of images with her phone and uploaded them to her platform as she walked. On and off, Anna's phone would vibrate and tell her that another notification was coming through. For the most part, she ignored it, knowing social media can often be fickle. Plus, Emily had a habit of texting her photos of her projects when she worked as a way to keep track of what parts or supplies she would need when they made their next trip into town. She was happy that her friend had found a new project.

Thanks to the multitude of broken windows, Anna knew she would be able to hear the contractor when he made it there. She didn't want to risk missing him and having power back on in the building. After over an hour of roaming through the house and with over three hundred images now saved on the camera, she emerged into the warm sunlight and made a beeline for the van and camper now parked in front of the garage where two large trees and a grassy lawn would make for the perfect outdoor kitchen setup. She loved that Emily could find the best spot, no matter where they were calling home at the moment.

Wanting to do her part, she set down the camera and her phone and started assembling their outdoor desks and picnic table. It didn't take long before she was rolling down the mosquito nets and giving the outdoor floor mat one final sweep. Just as she finished up and sat in her lawn chair with her phone and a beer, Emily emerged from the garage. She wiped off her hands and went to the mini-fridge, grabbed a brew, and sat down next to Anna. Anna unlocked her phone as they drank, and she almost spit out the frothy concoction when she saw the number of notifications.

"Holy cow," she stammered.

"What?" Emily asked.

"Take a look at our views! I started uploading pictures from my phone. Nothing great, but this is insane. Two separate images have already racked up fifty-thousand likes, and we've gained two thousand new subscribers in under two hours," Anna said.

"What? There is no way. It must be a glitch or something," Emily said.

Anna shook her head even as her friend pulled out her own phone to see for herself. It didn't take long for Emily's jaw to drop in complete shock. Though they had both anticipated their new adventure drawing some attention, nothing could have prepared them for the near-instant success of the estate. It was wonderful to know they were going to be able to make something not only out of their blogging but from the house as well. It was the perfect boost to keep them going after the run-in with Nancy earlier that day. She could be as angry as she wanted, but in the end, it wouldn't deter Emily and Anna from doing so.

"This is insane…those pictures aren't even that great, no offense, but we've posted images that we've spent hours editing, and they haven't gotten this sort of attention. Do you know what this means?" Emily asked.

"That we might actually be able to afford the renovations on this place?"

"That we've got a steady and proven stream here. We've got to jump on this right away. Let's go back through and get some video footage—"

"Whoa, take it easy now. Don't forget, we are in a marathon, not a sprint. We've got to pace ourselves. The word is spreading about this place, and we need to keep it slow and steady, at least until we know more."

Emily groaned. "I hate it when you are reasonable and make perfect sense."

She laughed. "I promise we are going to be able to do some amazing things with this place. I just want to make sure that we're doing it the right way. We haven't gone through the house yet, and even if the family members are all dead and gone, I want to try to keep anything personal or private of theirs off camera."

"See now, this is why you are so awesome. I never would have thought of that. My dad was right; you've got a good sense of staying out of trouble."

"Ha! I don't think your dad believes either of us has a single lick of sense after buying this place. He sees it as a money pit, and you know it."

"Yeah, but he's happy we are staying put for a while, so we've got that going for us," Emily said.

She smiled at her friend as they went back to the afternoon brews and read over the new onslaught of comments that their posts were getting. It was crazy to think that just a few days before, they were trying to decide what the next "hook" would be and how they could bring in more readers and views. Everything was different now. Now, it seemed as though the haunting estate was the answer to those prayers. As she gazed up at the massive structure, a chill moved through her, and Anna prayed they were making the right decision.

19

After twenty minutes of relishing in the cool, shaded space, a white truck with a contractor's logo pulled into the driveway. It was followed by a county utility van. The friends rose to greet the visitors as two men emerged in utility uniforms. Peter was followed by his son, Justin. There was no denying the two were related. Their features were similar in a dozen different ways. The teen was obviously fascinated by the estate, a detail that made Anna smile. She was hoping to bring that same wonderment to the rest of the world as well.

"Hi there," Anna said. "Boy, are we happy to see you guys."

Peter grinned. "Well, we are just tickled pink to be out here. I know the wiring in the garage is good to go, so if one of you wants to point the utility guys in the right direction, we can start on the house," he said.

Emily jumped into action right away, leading the two utility workers to the garage. She was anxious to have the power back on now that everything was set up in the van and camper. With the garage power on, they would be able to stop relying on the generator and solar power to keep things running and cool. While using solar was always their first choice, it was hard to find a reliable spot in the sun to make it a steady stream of power for their lifestyle. Instead, whenever possible, they'd hook into the system. Walking with Peter toward the house, she listened as he rattled off his credentials.

"I still can't get over the surprise when I got the call about this place. I didn't think anyone would ever have the resources to sink back into it. Hell, the knob and tube wiring is enough to send most running for the hills."

"Boy," Anna muttered. "You sure know how to make a girl worry…"

He grinned. "Sorry, I didn't mean to frighten you. All I'm saying is that if it's done right, not everything is going to need replaced. An electrician driven by the all-powerful dollar will see the work and tell you to rip everything out and start from scratch."

"And what do you think?" she asked.

"A good part of it needs to be replaced along with the breaker box, and that's just on the electrical part. However, there is a good bit of wiring that can stay in place, at least for now. I know we are talking about a huge project here."

"Oh boy, I'm starting to have second thoughts about this."

"Don't, not at all. Listen, this place is special not just for me but for so many other locals in the area. I think that we'll be able to work something out. I know all about the auction, and I don't think that the town was forthcoming enough with the work that needed to be done. I can't do much about that now, but I can promise to be fair about the costs and work with you on payments to make it happen."

"Listen, I appreciate the offer, but I don't want you to put yourself out. Heck, I just appreciate you coming out. We've got no idea what we're doing, but we do love this place."

"And that's why I'm happy to do it. It needs some love, and I can tell you're going to be here to give it to the old beast. That's all the assurance I need that I'm doing the right thing."

Anna was thrilled by the man's generosity. Not only was he willing to help them restore the estate to its former glory, but he was also going to work on a payment plan with them. Given the fleeting but bitter interactions they'd had with the locals so far, it was a pleasant surprise. She only hoped that Peter wouldn't change his mind when he realized that Nancy and a handful of others weren't exactly on their side now that they planned to live there and restore the property. One by one, they went through the rooms as he talked with her about what would need to be done. Some of them weren't so bad off, while others had sustained water damage and wouldn't be livable without a complete renovation.

In the end, she was happy Peter was the one who had taken on the job. Just as they emerged from the house, she saw the garage lights flicker to life and knew Emily had been successful in her mission as well. For the first time, it felt like they were making some progress on the property. After Peter had promised that he'd be starting work that same week, she was delighted with the outcome. Waving the utility crew and the contractors back down the driveway, Anna smiled as they returned to their outdoor kitchen, which was now running off the grid and not their generator. She grinned at Emily.

"Can you believe it?" Anna asked. "I never thought we'd be able to get started on this place so soon. It is like a dream come true. I hope Peter is as good as he seems."

"Well, I didn't see a ring on his finger, so maybe you could get us a little extra family discount…"

She snorted. "Get your mind out of the gutter, girl. He's got a teenage son. His wife passed away in childbirth. Plus, he's a little too old for me. I'm just happy he's so nice and wants to see this place brought back to life."

"Same. Now, hopefully, Lori doesn't bail on our plans. I want to show her around this place."

"Oh, I bet you do," Anna said.

"Now, whose mind is in the gutter?" Emily asked. "Don't worry; slow and steady will win this race. I'm not going to make a move on Lori."

"No? Whoa. I'll believe that when I see it."

"Hey now, believe it or not, I do have some self-control. Plus, I like her, and I don't want her to think I'm the type of woman who loves them and leaves them."

"Wait a minute, you mean you're not? When did that happen? Wow…you'd think I'd notice hell freezing over like that," Anna said.

The pair both laughed together, a comfortable silence falling between them as they looked out over the property. It was a work of art. No matter what the costs, Anna knew she had found her home at the estate. Even if the day came when Emily wanted to carry on down the road, something deep in Anna's heart told her she was already putting down roots at the forgotten mansion. Anna couldn't help but feel as though fate or something else was watching over her. For a flicker of a moment, something in the top windows caught her gaze, but when Anna looked, nothing was there. She tried to forget about it, but the house continued to call out to her, begging her to walk through the hauntingly silent halls and feel the presence there.

20

"Now, hold on, are you telling me that you've been here for five years and never once made it this close to the house?" Emily asked.

Lori shook her head. "Nope. I did try climbing over the fence one night after a few too many glasses of wine—"

"Whoa! A trespasser!"

"*Tried*. I was way too tipsy to make it very far, and considering it was the Fourth of July, the entire town was in the field, just down the street, watching fireworks. It was not my finest moment. Our local sheriff came and 'escorted' me back to the group. I think it was the single most humiliating moment of my life here…"

There was a chorus of laughter, but it was short-lived as they once more dug into the feast that Lori had brought with her a half hour before. They were all getting along without any problems, which was easy to understand, given Lori's laid-back and easy-going demeanor. Anna found herself liking the woman more and more as time went on. The number of similarities between Lori and Emily was uncanny.

"I told the officer I was just trying to channel my inner Claymont, to give back to the people, but he didn't believe me," Lori said.

"Nice," Emily replied. "So, I take it this Claymont fellow was liked by the locals?"

"*Liked?* Oh no, they downright adored him, and it's easy to understand why. Back in his day, old Claymont went out of his way to make sure that the townspeople had everything they needed."

"Really? What do you mean?" Anna asked.

"Anything. You name it, and he gave it to them. If someone's house was being repossessed, he'd pay it off for them. If they needed a new car, Claymont was your man. His generosity was known by just about everyone."

"I bet people took advantage of him a lot," Emily said.

Lori shook her head. "Only his own family. Anyone else he helped always went on to return the favor. Heck, the man who owns the market in town will tell you as much. His old man got cancer about two decades ago, and Claymont paid for the treatment, a temporary manager at the business, and a bunch of other stuff to help him get by. Now, even decades later, Claymont is honored by the shop owner's son. Every year, he gives out about fifty-thousand dollars in groceries to the local homeless shelters in the area."

"Wow, so people did like this guy then? I wonder why we haven't heard about him until now," Anna said.

"Everything he did was pretty local. I don't think he liked the attention. So, for the most part, his name and his charity work were kept out of the local papers. After he died, most people just carried on with whatever good deeds Claymont had started in the area, and before long, it became part of the fabric of this place."

"Did he ever have any kids? You mentioned his own family was kind of not the greatest," Emily said.

Lori nodded. "Yep, he had two sons, and boy, oh boy, there was drama when Claymont passed on back in the day. From the way the story goes, he buried his treasure to keep them from fighting over it and getting it all."

Anna snorted. "A buried treasure, you say?"

"I know, I know, I sound like I'm crazy, but listen, that man was stupid rich, like oil tycoon level of rich, and when he died, his accounts were empty. He'd cleaned them out not even three months before his death," Lori said.

"Yeah, but like you told us, he gave away a ton,

right? Maybe by the time he died, there was just nothing left of it. Isn't it possible that his charity work simply depleted the coffers?" Emily asked.

"I'm telling you, the man was crazy rich. Even if he'd spent most of it, there would be at least fifty million dollars just lying around. Of course, that was decades ago, so now it would be worth way more than that, but he was loaded. His sons raised hell about it, too, tried to say the nurses stole it—"

"Really?" Anna gasped. "Wow. What a great pair of kids. I kinda see why he didn't want them to get it."

"You and a lot of other people. They were ticked off and tore this place up top to bottom, but the will was clear. No one with Harrington blood was able to demolish this place. It's right there in black and white, framed in the middle of the town hall. There was even an article in the state paper about the obscurity of the will."

"Whoa, I guess his sons had good reason to be mad. Can you imagine your father not only telling you that you're not getting a dime, but he hid the money, and no one is allowed to wreck the house to find it? I bet they were livid," Anna said.

"Oh yeah, even their descendants come out of the woodwork on occasion to try to contest the will, but nothing ever comes from it. It was designed to keep this place standing and keep it out of the hands of Claymont's bloodline," Lori said.

"Boy, I don't know how I would feel if my father did that to me," Emily said.

She chuckled. "Your father would never cut you off, and if he did or even tried, your mother would skin him alive. Face it, you're a good daughter and not nearly as rotten as you claim."

"Hey now, don't go ruining my bad reputation," Emily said. "I like to think I'm just rebellious enough to stand out but not so much that my father feels the need to disown me."

As the conversation fell silent, each of them working on a different dish from the spread laid out on the table, she couldn't help but ponder what it all meant. There had to be a good reason people believed that Claymont would hide his fortune. Granted, the times had changed, and now it was easy to keep kids from getting an inheritance, but back in the day, she could only imagine the challenges that the family patriarch faced with his decision. Somehow, it made her appreciate the man and his home all the more.

Her attention soon turned from the food to the looming project that towered over them fifty feet away. She could almost feel the house watching her and waiting for their next move, but it was going to be a slow process. With each step they took toward restoration, Anna had to know she was keeping the original heart of the home. The last thing she wanted to do was bring in a modern influence that not only would their visitors hate, but she would feel as though she was dishonoring the history of the estate as well. Before long, Emily and Lori were setting off on an evening stroll around the property, and though she'd been invited along, Anna knew her friend wanted some time alone with Lori.

Given how exhausting the last few days had been, she was happy leaving them on their own while she packed up the leftovers and cleaned the outside eating area. Though they hadn't seen much wildlife since their arrival, Anna was certain the critters would come out as soon as it got dark. A misplaced bag or loaf of bread could spell disaster for them if it was left in the wrong area. Once, in Colorado and early in their travels, they hadn't taken the bear sighting notices seriously and woke to find the scavengers had destroyed not only a month's worth of groceries but a few thousand dollars in supplies as well. It was a hard lesson learned and a mistake they had not once made again.

For the first time in years, though, as she prepared to head into the camper and turn in for the night, Anna felt like she was settling down at home. A smile moved across her lips, though in her heart, she couldn't shake the feeling that someone was watching her. One last time, before heading for bed, Anna looked around their new home but saw nothing out of place. Maybe someday the chills would stop, but for that moment in time, Anna was happy, knowing it was likely just in her head.

21

With everything coming together, Anna felt as though everything was working to their advantage. They had a new friend in Lori, and they were already in the process of starting the work that needed to be done to the mansion. The entire vibe gave off a carefree feeling. It left her considerably more relaxed than she had anticipated. Hours after the laid-back dinner, Anna was able to fall asleep almost immediately after climbing into bed. She was hoping that within a few days, they would be able to ditch the camper and start moving things into the house, even though they didn't have much in the way of belongings. As soon as she closed her eyes, she drifted into a peaceful sleep at first. She was aware of the dreams she was having when a noise and movement of the camper caused her to bolt upright in bed.

What she felt startled her, and the dreams she was

continuing to have each night had her waking up in a cold sweat. Anna's heart was racing as she looked around the camper, but whatever had caused her to wake up was gone. It almost felt as though someone was climbing into the side of the camper, but the door was closed and locked, as they had grown accustomed to doing over the years of travel. The sudden movement from her rising in bed obviously woke up her friend, who had been sound asleep next to her. Emily rubbed her eyes and stared at her for a moment before saying a word.

"Is everything all right?"

"I thought I heard something, and it startled me."

Emily chuckled. "I didn't hear anything other than you jumping out of bed. We can go take a look around if you'd like."

Anna shook her head. "I don't think that'll be necessary. I'm sure it has something to do with the strange dreams I was having. I'll be fine. You can go back to sleep. I'm sorry I woke you up."

"No worries. Try not to think about your dreams too much."

As Emily lay back down and rolled over, Anna knew it was going to be impossible to forget what she was dreaming. Ever since their arrival in the area, she had been having several strange dreams. There was one reoccurring, and it always ended with her being chased through the house. Even as she tried to push all the thoughts out of her mind and focus on getting some rest, she understood it wasn't normal to have the dreams that had been haunting her each night. Luckily for her, she was finally able to start focusing on all the work that was going to need to be done on the estate and was soon fast asleep.

BY THE TIME Anna woke up the next morning, she was feeling much better. After she had finally been able to get back to sleep the second time, she slept peacefully. She had no idea what was causing the dreams she had been having, but she was thankful that, for most of the night, she had been able to sleep without any issues. Emily was already awake by the time Anna had gotten herself out of bed, and she was quietly and patiently waiting for the coffeepot to finish when she spotted the woman outside of the camper. The smell of the fresh brewing coffee made her senses tingle, and even though she was more rested than she had been in the past few days, there was nothing better than waking up to a cup of coffee.

Anna closed the door behind her and sat in one of the fold-out chairs already beside the door. Emily smiled at her before pouring a cup of coffee for each of them. After putting one cube of sugar in each cup, her friend stirred them both and handed her one of them. She thanked her before taking her first sip, and she was already anxious to get the day started. After a couple of drinks of coffee and enjoying the peaceful morning she had woken up to, she started thinking about the things they needed to get done that day. She took another sip before setting her cup down and smiling at Emily.

"It's nice to see you finally got some sleep," Emily said.

"I wasn't sure it was going to be possible with the way my dreams were affecting me last night. They have just seemed so real over the past few nights, but I'm sure it's mainly because of all the excitement."

"I wouldn't doubt it. Why don't you go ahead and tell me about the dream? Maybe there's some hidden meaning behind it."

Anna sighed. "They are just so strange. Last night, the dream started off with me being trapped in the house. I had no idea where I was, but there was a man that ran right by me."

"Had you ever seen him before?"

"He didn't look familiar to me, but everything was happening fast. The first couple of dreams I had were about me being chased through the house, but this time, it was slightly different. I decided to follow the man and see where he was going."

Emily chuckled. "I'm assuming by the way you woke up last night that it didn't go that well."

"Well, as I crept through the house behind him, he was trying to lead me somewhere. I know it sounds kind of crazy, but I honestly felt like it was happening in real life. It's part of the reason I woke up in a cold sweat."

"I thought it was because you heard something and felt the camper moving?"

"The movie might have been me tossing and turning in bed, but the dream was just so strange that I had to wake myself out of it. I followed him until he led me to a cubby in one of the rooms. It was a hidden place that seemed to have gone untouched for years, but when I climbed inside, there was a body hidden in it."

"Did you know sometimes dreams manifest themselves in a way that tells us something we didn't know?"

"What do you mean?"

"Sometimes, whether we realize it or not, our dreams can tell us something we had no idea we actually knew. Maybe you actually read something on the internet about this place, and our conversation about hidden passages and things like that simply brought to life your dream."

"I don't know about all that, although it seemed more realistic than most of the dreams I have ever had before."

"Maybe we should take that as a hint to go looking for the hidden room?"

Anna just chuckled at first before she realized Emily was serious. Emily was looking for some kind of adventure to get them through the day, and with all the stories they had heard about hidden treasures and gold, she wasn't sure it was a bad idea. She thought about the worst thing that could happen, and even though she didn't honestly believe there was a body hidden in the house, she wondered what kind of secrets the mansion was keeping from the rest of the world. She had a feeling the dreams weren't just a manifestation of her imagination but that the house itself was trying to tell her something.

It was the same way she felt after the first dream she'd had, but Anna wasn't sure how to feel about it all. While she had some supernatural theories due to the novels she had written in the past, she had never fully believed in all of them. Some things were plausible, even if the majority of people around the world denied it. As she looked into the eyes of her friend, who was patiently waiting for an answer, she knew there would be little harm in searching the house again for hidden passages. At the very least, it gave her another reason to go looking for a treasure she felt had been found years ago. One of her favorite things to do was leave her friend sitting on the edge of her seat. So, rather than answering Emily immediately, Anna leaned forward in her chair and picked up her cup of coffee. Taking a long sip and making slurping noises on purpose, she waited for Emily to sigh dramatically.

When that moment finally came, Anna grinned and set the cup back down. As soon as she nodded in agreement that the search was going to happen, Emily jumped up with excitement. She had given her friend the right answer, but the only thing she could do was sit in her chair and smile. A thought crossed her mind, and she started to wonder if they had any chance of finding the fortune supposedly hidden inside the house. If they did, she thought about what they would do with all the money.

22

Anna gave herself a few minutes to finish her coffee, all the while thinking about how nice it would be to recover a fortune from a house they had gotten at such a low cost. She had never had that kind of luck, but it never stopped her from imagining what it would feel like to be rich. Although she was trying to wake up and remember the direction the dream had taken her through the house, Emily was already putting on her shoes and getting ready for their new adventure. Knowing it was only a matter of time before Emily would be begging Anna to start looking, she finished off the rest of her morning coffee and put her own shoes on before the two of them headed in the direction of the front door.

Again, as they walked toward the front porch of the mansion, with Anna leading the way, she got the feeling they were being watched. She stopped for just a moment when they reached the door, looking around to see if she could spot anyone on the property, but there was nothing to be seen. The feeling sent a shiver down her spine, and she wondered if she would ever feel comfortable in their new setting. Shaking all the thoughts from her mind and pushing forward, Anna opened the front door and stepped inside. There was something different when she walked in that time, but she couldn't put her finger on it. Before she had the chance to think about the situation for a moment longer, she heard Emily chuckling behind her.

"What is so funny?"

"I was just thinking about how we practically got this place for nothing. Wouldn't it just be crazy to find out that there is a hidden passage, and on top of that, we come across a dead body inside?"

"I don't think that would be funny at all," Anna said. "The only thing that would do is make me question every dream I have ever had."

Emily shook her head. "You know what I'm saying. It would definitely put a twist on everything that has happened to us. I'm not saying I am hoping we do find anything like that, but it would be screwed up if we did."

"Now *that* I can agree with."

"So, any idea which room we are headed to?"

"The dream is kind of fuzzy in my memory, but I know it was one of the bedrooms."

"Upstairs we go," Emily said with a smile on her face.

While Anna was glad Emily was enjoying herself, she couldn't help but think about the idea that they might actually find a body. It was the last thing she wanted to think about, and as they made their way upstairs, Anna couldn't shake the feeling that they were doing something wrong. With each step she took, the memory of her dream the night before was becoming clearer. She had no idea which room they needed to be headed to in order to find the secret passage from her dream, but she was sure that, based on the look of the room, it had been the master suite. They checked each room along the way before finally finding the one that looked as though it could have been the one from Anna's dream.

Emily started feeling along the wall while she made her way to the headboard and looked behind it. In her dream, the man had moved the bed away from the wall and pulled something out before doing something else that actually opened up the secret passage. When Emily realized what Anna was doing, she crossed the room and went to the other side of the bed before they both pulled it away from the wall. She felt a loose piece of board when she brushed her hand against it, and Anna pulled out a four-inch piece of it. She was shocked when she took a closer look and realized there was a small keyhole behind the board she had just removed.

"I was just joking when I thought we might actually find something," Emily said.

"I-I don't know what to say. There's a keyhole here, but I don't know where to find the key that goes into it."

"Do you remember anything else from your dream?"

"I remember he did something to the headboard before pulling out something."

"Maybe the key is hidden somewhere in the headboard, then?"

Anna started feeling around the top of the headboard before finding a small piece of trim that looked as though it could be movable. As soon as she reached for the board and laid her fingertips across the top, it started to slide away and revealed a key inside. Grabbing a hold of it and pulling it out, she looked down at the key in shock. For just a moment, thoughts of every dream she had ever had in her life started to fill her mind. It was impossible to think that the dream from the night before was the only one she'd had that was accurate, and looking down at the key she had in her hand, she had never seen it before.

She was left speechless for several minutes, and even though she could hear her friend say something, it felt as though she was the only one in the room. Anna looked from the key back to the keyhole before her eyes traveled slowly up to her friend. Emily was standing just a couple of feet away, and although she could see the woman's mouth moving, Anna couldn't hear anything. Finally, she was able to push all of her thoughts to the side and focus on Emily's words.

"I don't think you had a dream last night at all," Emily said. "I didn't believe we were actually going to find anything, but I thought it would be fun to look."

"If it wasn't a dream, then what was it?"

"I bet you had some kind of premonition about this place. Maybe it's from all the stories we've been looking up, or you somehow managed to recall something someone had said. Either way, I'm starting to wonder if we should call the police."

Anna sighed. "I'm hoping this is just some sort of wild coincidence. Let's not worry about getting the police involved until we know what's on the other side of this passage. Do you believe we're going to find a body on the other side?"

Emily shrugged. "There's no telling what we are going to find on the other side. We had no idea that this even existed."

"I just don't want it to be the same as my dream."

"So far, everything is lined up with what you told me. Are you sure you don't want to call the police first?"

"Let's just see what we find. I don't want to be the woman in town who called the police over every strange occurrence."

In the back of her mind, even though the dream had led them to where they were standing, Anna thought she was going to place the key into the hole and that the opening was going to be right behind the bed. Instead, when she placed the key into the keyhole and turned it, the fireplace on the other side of the room started to groan, and one side popped free. There was a feeling of relief that washed over her, knowing the dream she'd had the night before didn't get everything right. It was possible that the entire situation was a coincidence and nothing more. They both made their way across the room and tugged on the open side of the fireplace at the same time.

It had obviously been a long time since the secret passage had been used, and they were struggling to pull the hidden doorway away from the wall. When it finally started to give, it opened, causing them both to fall to the floor. Emily immediately started laughing, and Anna joined in as well. After pulling themselves up to their feet and walking back to the secret door, they both looked inside. The small space behind the fireplace wasn't very big, but there was something reflecting in the corner of the cubby that caught her eye. Her heart dropped. Stashed between the back of the fireplace and the walls of the small closet-sized room behind it, hidden from the world, was a stack of dust-covered gold bars. A sight she had only seen in movies.

23

Anna was shocked by what she saw. Although they had heard several stories about there being treasure hidden somewhere throughout the house, she never actually thought they would find it. For just a moment, the two of them stood in silence in front of the open passageway. It was impossible to believe that a dream had led them to a fortune, but she had no other choice but to start thinking it was possible. Somehow, the dream that had woken her up from a deep sleep the night before had brought them to a pile of gold bars stacked on top of each other. There was just enough light coming through the window that allowed them to see the glimmering corners of a few of the bars. The amount of dust sitting on top of them told her they had been there for quite some time.

She pulled out her phone and turned on the flashlight, shining it into the darkness within the cubbyhole. As soon as the light hit the gold bars, the reflection lit up the entire room that had been hidden behind the fireplace. Anna had a thought that caused her to wonder if the gold bars were even real, and she stepped forward into the passageway and picked up one of the chunks of metal. It was much heavier than she had anticipated, and she ended up having to use both hands to lift it. As far as she could tell, they were as real as the gold bars at Fort Knox. There hadn't been a single time in her life she had held such beauty in her hands, and it felt as though her heart was going to stop. It took several seconds to realize that her friend was talking to her again, and she glanced up in the woman's direction.

"What did you say?"

"I said there has to be millions of dollars in gold in here if it is actually real," Emily replied.

Anna nodded. "Honestly, I have no idea if it's real or not, but I can say they are much heavier than they look. What in the world are we supposed to do with it now?"

"I think the first thing we need to do is get this pile of gold bars someplace safe."

She chuckled. "As far as all the rumors we've been told, this gold has been sitting here untouched for over sixty years. The safest place it can be is right here, where we found it."

"That's true. What if we just take one of the gold

bars for now and head into the city to get it authenticated? Maybe one of the jewelry stores or something like that will be able to give us an idea of whether it's real or not."

"That's a good idea."

"If we find out that it's real, then I will get ahold of my father, and he will be able to help us figure out what to do next."

"Do you think he would be able to help us figure out the next step?"

Emily nodded. "If there is anyone in this world who can help us out, I know it's going to be him. The first thing we need to do is find out if this is even real or not."

Anna thought about the consequences they would face if the gold turned out to be real. Not only would they be rich, but she wondered how many people would come out of the woodwork to try to claim it. She had no idea how the laws worked when it came to possessing such a fortune, but she could remember television shows she had watched in the past and the struggle people had to go through in order to get the money from such a fortune. She was amazed by how heavy the gold bar was in her hand, and as soon as she handed it to Emily, Anna could tell she was in shock as well. Neither one of them had held such richness before, and she was trying to figure out what they would do if the gold bars turned out to be real.

With the help of Emily, who was holding one of the gold bars in her hand, they closed the secret passageway. Anna made her way to the bed and put everything back where she had found it, aside from the key, which she placed in her pocket. Throughout the entire process, her heart was racing. She wasn't sure if they had found a fortune behind the fireplace or if they were going to be fooled by some prank that had been over sixty years in the making. Either way, as she placed the piece of trim back where she had found it, they were in for an exciting story to share with the world. Once they had both made sure that everything looked exactly as it had when they had entered the room, they started making their way back down the hallway and toward the staircase that would take them downstairs.

"What's your initial reaction to all of this?" Emily asked.

Anna chuckled. "I want to be excited about it, but I don't know if this is real gold or not. I can't imagine that no one has found it in so many years."

"You have to admit it was a perfect hiding place. It took you having a premonition to be able to find it, and maybe Claymont wanted to keep it that way."

"You don't think that a spirit helped me find it, do you?"

Emily shrugged. "Do you have any other way of explaining what just happened? I mean, Justin told me that his spirit was keeping his relatives from finding it. Maybe the spirit feels like you deserve it."

Anna laughed. "Isn't that a crazy thought? Some random woman from nowhere gets the property by luck, just to find a fortune in gold bars that no one else has ever been able to locate."

"I know it sounds incredibly crazy, but I honestly have no other way of explaining it."

As they made their way downstairs and out through the front door, Anna was left thinking about the possibility that a spirit had given her a map to a treasure that no one else had ever been able to find. The entire idea of it all was insane, but the more she thought about it, the more she realized she couldn't make sense of it any other way. The only thing she knew for sure was that they were holding a gold bar in their hands, and if it was real, there were many more of them upstairs in a hidden passageway. It was hard to believe they were possibly hours away from being millionaires, but she wasn't getting her hopes up.

Everything Anna had in her life she had because she had worked hard for it, and even though it wasn't a lot, she loved it all. It was never going to be easy for someone like her, and she didn't want to believe that the gold bar her friend was carrying was the answer they had been looking for all their lives. She did allow herself to dream momentarily as she thought about all the things they would be able to do with the money. However, until just a few days before, they were living out of their van and camper, she couldn't help but think about how much work they would be able to get done on the property. She was surprised by how much she felt like the mansion was already home, even if they hadn't slept inside a single night.

Anna thought about the rest of the life she'd had up to that point and how hard it had been throughout her childhood. Could it be possible that a spirit had decided she was worth a fortune? It was something she wasn't going to be able to answer, but she was hopeful the treasure they had found would change their lives forever. As she was thinking about all the things they would be able to do with the money, Emily was telling her all about how she couldn't wait to talk to her dad. Emily seemed to be a little more excited than Anna was about what they had found, while she was just hoping it was real.

There had been too many times in her life when she had thought things were going to change for the better, only for her to be kicked out of another foster home and moved once again. The last thing she wanted to do was get her hopes up. They had stumbled across a treasure that was going to change their lives, but it was hard not to think about the possibility. People all around the country would win the lottery, and it made her think about how finding out the gold was real was going to change her own life. The feeling of being watched from a distance washed over her as they walked out the front door and headed back toward the van. Anna turned around and was glad to see that Emily had covered the bar, even if she was carrying something heavy.

24

Three hours had passed since they had found the stack of gold bars, and they were sitting under the awning next to the camper. They had talked about several ideas on how to use the money if the gold was real, but Anna was trying to wrap her head around the fact that they had found it all. She had thought about the dream she'd had the night before, and she wasn't sure that a spirit could have somehow altered her thinking while she slept. There was simply no other way to explain how easily they had found the fortune, but she was holding some excitement back as they waited for Russ to call back. Emily had sent her father a message after calling. The man had sent a courier to their location to pick up the gold bar, and they had picked it up nearly an hour and a half before. They were simply waiting to hear back from her father at that point.

Anna and Emily had talked about keeping everything as low profile as possible, especially since so many people had looked for the fortune for so long. She remembered the markings on the gold bar they had found, wondering what the symbol meant. Without hesitation, she found herself sitting on the edge of her seat with anticipation. Even though she was trying to listen to half of the conversation, she could hear the words Emily was saying, but they didn't register. She was lost in thought and excitement about their find, but when she ended the call, she cleared everything else from her mind and focused on what the woman had to say.

"My dad said the courier arrived at his office an hour ago. We should have answers soon."

"Did he happen to say what his thoughts on it were? I mean, does he think the gold bar is real?"

Emily smiled. "Officially, he can't say whether the gold bar is real or not, but he's optimistic it is."

"I wonder what kind of process it has to go through in order to find out if it's real."

"I have no idea, but I think we are about to come into a lot of money."

Anna chuckled. "I don't think I have ever felt this excited about anything."

"That makes two of us, but I'm wondering about the symbol we found on the gold bar," Emily replied.

"I was just sitting here thinking about the same

thing before your dad called. I wonder if we can look up anything on the internet and find out."

Within seconds, they had both pulled out their laptops and started typing vigorously. Anna had no idea what exactly she was looking for, but she would recognize the symbol if she found a picture of it. She spent several minutes looking up different thoughts she had before she typed in the Harrington name. It immediately brought up a history of the town and the people who had settled in it years before. It didn't take long after that for her to find a picture of the family crest, and she realized that the fortune they had found was straight from the story they had been told about Claymont Harrington. She found herself staring at the symbol for several moments when she realized the gold bars had to be real. Before she allowed herself to get lost in thought for too long, she spun her laptop around and showed the picture to Emily, who immediately had the same look of shock on her face.

Her friend understood what she was looking at, and they both seemed to come to the same realization at the same time. They weren't going to have to wait for her father to respond. They both knew the gold was real. One way or another, they were about to be rich. Anna had no idea what a gold bar was worth or how many of them were upstairs in the hidden room, but it was going to be more than enough to do any renovations they could dream of to the property. It was a strange sensation to think about working on a home they didn't even know existed just a few days before, but she was suddenly excited about the future.

Once they had the information about the family crest, they both started to research the lore behind the fortune. Even though they were both excited by the idea that they were going to be coming into a lot of money, they were equally as excited about the story behind it. Anna knew it was because of the writer inside of her, but she couldn't wait to tell her fans and fellow bloggers about their find. It took some time, but she finally came across a story that seemed to go into a little more detail about the legend behind the gold. The main story she found was from a handful of people who claimed to have helped Claymont move the gold bars all those years before.

While it made for a good story, Anna found it hard to believe that people had helped him move the gold bars without knowing the exact location of where they had been moved. She wondered why a man was trying to keep a fortune from his family and wouldn't do all the work himself unless he had reached an age in his life that made it impossible for him to carry the heavy, precious metal. She found herself wondering how much a gold bar weighed and looked up the information in her search engine. The very first answer to her question was twenty-seven and a half pounds, and the photograph, along with it, looked to be the right size for the bars they had found. She tried to visualize the size of one of the gold bars and realized that the measurements were the same.

"Do you have any idea how many bars were up there?" Anna asked.

"I counted twenty before we left."

She whistled. "That's going to be a lot of money. It looks like, depending on the buyer, each one could be worth half a million dollars or more."

Emily's jaw dropped. She was just as shocked as Anna. Anna realized they had possibly gone from needing to make payments on the work that needed to be done to the estate to being able to pay cash for the renovations. She had no idea how to feel, but her emotions were going wild. Although she was almost certain the gold bars were real, they needed to wait to hear from Russ before they could get too worked up. As much as she wanted to be excited about the situation, and even though they had already done a lot of research on their own, Anna wasn't ready to get ahead of herself.

Anna knew throughout most of her life that things didn't work out for the better. There had been too many times in her life she had gotten excited about something only to be let down, and even though the current situation called for celebration, she wanted to know what Russ had to say about the authenticity of the gold bars before she allowed herself to do so. The man was the lead attorney and owner of a law firm in the city, and he would know exactly what they needed to do if the gold turned out to be real. When they ran into legal trouble during their stays across the country, he had been there for them.

The man was a wizard when it came to the law and had helped them out with several legal troubles they had found themselves in. They had never gotten themselves into much, but sometimes, they would try to camp out in locations that people didn't want them in. She could remember a time when he had flown across the country to help fight a legal battle with an unfriendly campground owner, only to get the case thrown out an hour after his arrival. Suddenly, almost as though she had wished it into existence, Emily's phone rang, and she put it on speaker so both of them could hear what he had to say.

"What did you find out, Dad?"

Russ laughed. "I wasn't sure you were telling the truth when you first called me, but I just got word that all of that gold is real. I've already sent out an armored truck to pick up the rest of it."

"Why do we need an armored truck?" Emily asked.

"Each one of those gold bars is worth nearly six hundred thousand dollars—maybe more. I'm not taking any chances of something happening between leaving the estate and getting it to my office."

"What do you want us to do?"

"As soon as you get the gold loaded up into the armored truck, I want you to follow it here. We will go over everything as soon as you're at the office with me."

25

Anna found it more difficult to contain her excitement. Although she was excited about the find, she was starting to feel something she had never felt before. They were going to have all the money they needed to fix up the mansion and the rest of the estate, but a thought popped into her mind that took away the majority of her excitement. She started to wonder if the Harrington family would have any claim to the fortune. After all, even though she was the rightful owner of the property and the estate, the family crest was printed on each bar. If the family who had been searching for the treasure for so long wanted to take it away from them, she wondered if there was any legal standing to do so. Luckily for her, Emily's father was on the phone.

"What about ownership of the gold?" Anna asked. "I'm thinking the Harrington family might have a claim to it since their family crest is imprinted on each bar."

"That's the main reason it took me so long to get back in touch with you," Russ said. "I've already looked over the contract that Emily sent over for the purchase of the home. It turns out that you are the only one who has any claim to the gold."

"How is that possible?"

"The town made sure they were free from any liability, considering the shape of the old house. In doing so, they made the sale contract bulletproof after both parties signed it. There's nothing anyone can do to take anything you find inside away from you."

"So, since the town was worried about any backlash they might receive if something happened to the new owner, they managed to sign any other rights away with the documents as well?" Emily asked.

"That's right. The mansion, the estate, the property, the gold, and anything else found on the property are yours rightfully. Not a single Harrington heir can come out of the woodwork and lay claim to it."

"Why would they do something like that? I mean, the contractor and his son made it sound like they come out every once in a while to search for the hidden treasure."

Russ chuckled. "They signed over every right they had to the property when they sold it to the county. Judging by the legal documents I have gone over from past sales, they just wanted to get every penny they could from the sale itself."

"So, they basically sold their rights to the treasure?"

"There's nothing making do at this point."

Hearing that there was no way anyone could come after them for the treasure they had found made her feel much better. Anna was finally allowing herself to enjoy the excitement she had been trying to contain all day. She had no idea how long the process was going to take before they would be able to sell any of the gold bars, but she knew any financial worries that either of them had were gone. The only thing they needed to focus on was getting the gold bars loaded up and meeting Russ at his office. Every worry she had about the Harrington family slowly faded away. When she woke up that morning, she had no idea that her entire life was going to change for a second time that week.

It was hard to believe that so many things were changing at once, but she knew each and every one of them was for the better. Anna couldn't remember the last time she had been so happy, and although she had enjoyed her life traveling the country by van, she was looking forward to seeing how the other side lived. As the gold bars that were sitting in their hiding place crossed her mind, she wondered what kind of lifestyle they were going to have once they were sold. Realizing that Russ was still on the other line, she thanked him for everything he had done up to that point. He replied that they needed to get the armored truck loaded as soon as it arrived and head out before telling them both he would see them soon. As soon as the call ended, Emily and Anna wrapped their arms around each other and laughed.

"What is going on?" Emily asked.

"What do you mean?"

"It seems like everything in the last week has changed our lives. I bought a couple of random tickets for this place, and we won. Now, we own a place we can finally call home, and we are about to be millionaires on top of it. Have you ever heard of such a change of luck?"

Anna shook her head. "I was just wondering the same thing."

"Do you find it that hard to believe that a spirit led the way?"

"I have no idea what to believe, but I'm happy we were the ones to find the treasure. This is going to change everything."

"You still want to renovate the mansion, right?" Emily asked.

"That's at the top of the list. It's hard to believe we have a place to call our own, but what are we going to do?"

Emily laughed. "I can tell you one thing we aren't going to do. We certainly aren't going to be making payments for the work Peter and Justin are going to be doing at the house. We are going to be able to pay for all the repairs in cash."

Anna started to smile, knowing Emily was right. She had already gone through the same thought process on her own, and things were going to change quite a bit in their lives. Knowing they were going to have to take the van to Russ's office, they started to pack up as much of their camping gear as they could. The van was attached to the camper since they had moved it closer to the garage in order to connect to a power source. It didn't take them long to prepare to leave, and a short time later, the armored truck arrived. At that point, it was difficult for either one of them to contain their excitement. They were bouncing off the walls as they carried the gold bars to the truck.

It was crazy to think about how much their lives were about to change, but she was excited about it for the first time. It was going to take a little time to process the change entirely, but by the time they were loading the last bar into the back of the truck, she knew their lives were never going to be the same. Anna was struggling to comprehend what it would all mean in the grand scheme of things, but for the first time in her life, she wasn't going to have to worry about finances anymore. Even as they climbed into the van and followed the armored truck down the driveway, she glanced back at the mansion and the rest of the property.

All the things they had been talking about when it came to their plans for the estate and the new bed and breakfast were going to be a lot easier now that they had the money to take care of it all. Emily was thinking about the same thing, even though neither of them were talking to the other. When her friend reached over and turned on the radio, a classic rock song was playing on the station. They started singing along together, knowing they were one step closer to not having a care in the world. They spent the entire trip following the armored truck, singing along to different songs. Anna couldn't wait to take the next step in their lives.

26

Nearly a week had gone by, and they had spent the entire time in the big city with Emily's father. Anna had never been the kind of person who enjoyed city life, but she'd had a good time with her friend, making sure that everything was lined up. Russ had gone out of his way to ensure the gold had sold for as much as they could get for it, even if she didn't understand the process they had to go through. But she was already looking forward to getting back to the estate she had grown so fond of.

The money from the sale of the gold was in her account, and she was stunned as she looked at the account information on her phone. Emily was driving the van back to the estate, and she was enjoying the idea that they no longer had to worry about money. Each of the twenty bars of gold had sold for six hundred thousand dollars, giving them just over twelve million dollars in their account. It was a figure she never imagined she would see unless she had a New York Times bestselling novel, but she was glad she got to share every penny of it with Emily. By the time they were pulling back up to the estate, Anna was excited to be able to start the project without having to make payments to Peter and Justin. They were going to be able to get the work done much quicker since they had the cash to purchase anything they needed.

Emily was parking the van by the camper when her phone started to ring. Anna grabbed her friend's phone and looked at the caller ID, happy to see it was Lori. The woman had called Emily several times during their absence, and Anna knew there was a romance starting to grow between the two of them. She was happy that her friend had finally found true love, but she was even more excited to be able to witness it firsthand. Without hesitating, she answered the call and placed it on speaker so Emily could hear it as she was backing the van into its parking spot.

"Are you guys back at the estate yet?" Lori asked.

"We are just pulling in now. What's going on?" Emily asked.

"I was just making sure we are still on for the interview for the town paper. I thought I could come over and interview both of you so I could get it written out for the newspaper as soon as possible."

"I was going to give you a call here in a few minutes to let you know we were back."

Lori chuckled. "That's a good story."

Emily laughed. "You should know by now I wasn't going to make you wait that long to get the interview."

"I know, but you are a lot of fun to mess with. When would be a good time for me to come over and interview both of you? I know everyone is dying to get to know the two women who struck it rich."

"Just give us a couple hours to get settled in, and then you are more than welcome to stop by."

"Sounds great. I'll see you then."

Anna ended the call just as Emily finished unpacking the van. It was hard to believe that so much had changed in such a short time frame as she climbed out of the van and looked in the direction of the front entrance. At Russ's request, they had hired a security company to keep an eye on the property twenty-four hours a day, seven days a week. She waved at the guard, who waved back. Although she had never been in a position where she needed to have security on hand, she felt safe with the guard posted out front. Emily's father had sent them a list of companies to use and made sure none of them were from around the area where the estate was located.

As she closed the door to the van, she glanced back at the mansion. Anna knew they would be staying in the van and camper for a little while longer, but she was happy to see that Peter and his crew had already started on several projects that needed to be done before they could get the power turned on. They had reached out to the man while they were in the city and sent him the down payment for his services. He had immediately started the project before their return. Anna was looking forward to seeing the transformation of the mansion as each project was completed, but she was even more excited to see the finished product.

Anna and Peter had emailed each other back and forth with different ideas for certain parts of the house that would suit their needs for the bed and breakfast they were planning to create. It was one of the things that kept her sane while she was in the city, but she was excited to be home again. She felt strange when she thought of the word home, but that was exactly where they were. She spotted Justin through one of the mansion windows and waved before he disappeared again. A few minutes after their arrival at the estate, Anna and Emily got to work setting up the camper and preparing it for them to live in once again. Although living in the van was something she had grown accustomed to, she was already looking forward to the first night they would be able to spend inside the house.

As the hours of the day started to trickle by, she watched the crew of construction workers move in and out of the house. Anna found it difficult not to go in every so often to check on the work, but she knew the surprise would be much better if she waited. Instead, she had tried to keep herself busy with her blog and sharing updates with her fans. She had attempted to get back to work on her next novel, but she was trying to piece together the story she wanted to tell. Meanwhile, Emily was busy working just a few feet away from her. As much as she didn't want to see much of the interior until it had been completed, Peter and Justin had asked for their opinions on multiple occasions.

She had given up on getting any writing done and was busy helping guide the man in the direction she wanted the project to go. Anna and Emily had also come to an agreement on the colors they were looking for, although they wanted to keep much of the woodwork as original as possible. The two of them were standing in the foyer, talking to a couple of the other workers, trying to decide what they wanted to do with one of the downstairs rooms. Although the crew only had a couple of days' head start before they returned, they were already making great strides. They weren't going to have to wait much longer before they could stay inside the mansion.

They had just been inside the house for a few minutes, discussing some ideas for the foyer and color scheme, when she heard a car pulling into the driveway. Anna wasn't expecting anyone until later, when Lori would be there to interview both of them for the town's newspaper. She made her way through the front door of the mansion and stepped out onto the porch, just in time to see a car flying up the driveway and come screeching to a stop. The woman driving was the mayor, but Anna didn't understand what was going on. When she heard someone walking up next to her, she glanced over to see Emily standing next to her with the same confused expression on her face.

Anna looked away from Emily and back to Nancy, who was climbing out of her car and storming in their direction. Although she had no idea what was happening, the woman was outraged about something. They hadn't spoken to Nancy since they had left to go to the city, but Anna simply thought the woman was upset about the construction for some reason. Whatever Nancy's problem was, Anna already had her phone ready to call Russ at a moment's notice. He warned them that some of the members of the town might not agree with them being the rightful owners of the gold and told each of them to contact him immediately if someone tried to lay claim to it.

27

"Just what the hell is going on?" Nancy demanded.

Anna shrugged. "Just getting everything started on the work that needs to be done on the house."

"That's not what I'm talking about, and you know it. Rumor has it that the two of you have found the family fortune."

As much as she hated city life, Anna had always hated the fact that small towns always seemed to know everyone else's business. She was pretty sure that Harrington was no different than any other small town and that every resident in the area probably knew what they had for breakfast each and every day. Anna was slightly taken aback by how the mayor was reacting, but she wasn't about to give the woman any information about her personal finances. Russ had warned her to keep the fortune a secret, even though it was going to be hard to do with the amount of work that needed to be done on the property. Taking a deep breath, she exhaled slowly. The last thing she wanted to do was make an enemy out of the town's mayor.

"My finances are personal, and I don't think you have any right to ask me about them."

The woman scoffed. "I'm not asking about your finances, but if you were somehow able to find the fortune, you need to tell me immediately."

"I don't need to tell you anything."

"That's not true. If you find the gold hidden away in the house, then you need to tell me immediately. The gold is historical, and it being found would void the sale of the estate."

Anna shook her head. "That's not even remotely true. I've already had my attorney look over all the documents and the contract. There's nothing you can do with anything we happen to find here."

"So, you did find the gold. That means the sale of the estate was illegal and needs to revert back to the county ownership immediately."

"I don't know what you're trying to pull here, but my attorney has already looked over the contract, and there's nothing you can do. Besides, the gold is already gone and has been processed."

"Are you kidding me? This is an outrage. I can assure you that the contract is null and void. I'm going to need the contact information for your attorney. You can't just sell something that doesn't belong to you, and it certainly can't be legal that you're spending my money."

Not only did the statement send a shockwave through her, but she was entirely confused by the way the woman was acting. Nancy was acting as though all the fortune was hers, even though the contract for the sale was legally binding and there wasn't anything that could be done to change it. Russ was one of the best attorneys in the country, and there wasn't a single loophole that Nancy could use to get any of the money from the sale of the gold.

Although Anna was trying to keep herself composed and not anger the woman any further, Nancy was starting to get belligerent. Anna wasn't able to wrap her mind around what was going on when the woman stepped forward and was directly in her face. Anna had been ready to call Russ at a moment's notice, but instead, she reached into her pocket and pulled out one of the business cards that her friend's father had given them in case of an emergency dealing with legal matters. Her friend's father hadn't made them make a single payment for his services, but he would be more than happy to take care of what they were dealing with.

Nancy was going on about something, and although Anna was more than aware that the woman was threatening her with taking the property back,

Anna knew it wasn't going to be possible. She let the woman go on for several more moments before she finally had enough. After taking another deep breath, she sighed and extended the card in the woman's direction. She wasn't about to deal with the anxiety starting to fill her mind. The rage building inside her was more than what she wanted to express, and she simply forced a smile instead, hoping to anger the woman in her own way.

"What is this?"

Anna scoffed. "You said you wanted the information for my attorney, and I'm giving it to you."

"This isn't going to be the last you hear of me. I can assure you I am going to take this to the highest court possible."

"Until you do, you can leave me alone. This is my attorney's business card, and if you have any questions, you can make sure they go through him. I'm not about to have you standing on my property and threatening to take what is rightfully mine."

"Rightfully yours?" the woman snapped. "The family fortune belongs to me and my family. Just knowing you found it is more than enough for me to make sure the sale of the property is voided."

"Again, you can take that up with my attorney. Now, if you would please get the hell off of my property, I'm not about to be bullied by you."

"We could have done this the easy way, but I see

that you would much rather do this the hard way. I'm going to make you regret not playing nice."

Anna was shocked by the way the woman was acting, but she was sure it was simply out of jealousy since they had been the ones to find the treasure. She hadn't wanted to divulge the information that they had indeed found the gold everyone had been looking for, but she knew there was nothing anyone could do about it. The last thing she was going to deal with was someone standing on her property, threatening her. As Nancy started to turn around and storm back to her car, Anna was relieved she was no longer going to have to be the one listening to her voice. Russ would take care of everything from that point on. Anna already knew the contract for the estate was legally binding, and it was too late to go back on any of it.

They had spent the entire first day in the city listening to the man go over all the legalities involved with the contract. Although she hadn't understood most of it at the time, Emily's father had done a great job of making sure he explained everything in great detail. Anna knew it was only because he wanted to make sure they were prepared for everything and anything, but she was thankful enough that she wasn't going to have to deal with Nancy or anyone else who might come along. As the woman climbed into her car and started to speed down the driveway, Anna looked back at Emily and shrugged.

"What the hell was that about?"

"I have no idea, but you might want to give your father a call and warn him about what might be coming his way."

Emily smiled and nodded. "I'm sure it won't take much for him to put her in her place, but I never expected her to act that way."

"Neither did I. I'm just as shocked as you are."

It was at that moment that she started to think about what the woman had actually said. Nancy said it wasn't right that Anna was spending *her* money, and it made Anna wonder what she meant by her statement. Anna wondered if the mayor wanted the money for herself and what that would mean for the Harrington family. She knew, since the county had legal ownership of the property before the sale, that the woman probably just wanted it for the town. It was the only answer she had, but she found herself wondering how far she would be able to take the fight. Under the best of circumstances, Russ was going to have his hands full with the attitude she had just received.

28

"Hooray!" Emily exclaimed.

The pop of the champagne bottle's cork felt like she was releasing all the pressure that had been building inside of her. Two days had passed, and in that time, the construction crew and the friends had been working non-stop. It was hard to believe they finally had power in the house. That detail in itself was impressive, given how much needed to be done. Peter and his team had jumped into the project with both feet and enthusiasm. The result had been power in under forty-eight hours. Not only was she impressed, but she was also overcome with joy.

Though it was nowhere near ready for the general public, two of the rooms that shared a bathroom had been repaired enough to be deemed livable. They had once more gotten lucky in that the rooms were the least damaged in the house, with somewhat reliable plumbing running to the shared bathroom. With that in mind, the women had already decided to move into the house when the lights came back on. Each day they stayed in the van and camper, they added unnecessary wear and tear to the space. Anna poured them both a glass of the bubbly while Emily tossed a towel on the floor where it had spilled over.

"I can't believe we are actually staying here now. Look at this place! Your room is bigger than the van and camper combined. You've got a sitting room...in your bedroom," Emily said.

"I know it's insane. Your room is the same size, though, goofball. I don't know where I want to start decorating and doing the work that needs to be done. The floors need to be sanded and varnished, but I can't wait to replace this ugly wallpaper," Anna said.

"Well, here's hoping our good luck keeps holding out and we'll have the plumbing moving through the whole house soon. Peter said he's got at least three lines to replace."

"But the septic system is in good shape, thank God, so if rusted pipes are our biggest problem, I'm going to count us as lucky."

"Yeah, I couldn't agree more. So, what do you say? We finish this bottle, check out the lights in the rooms, then get unpacked?" Emily asked.

Anna nodded in agreement before they clinked their glasses and started drinking. Though it was the third time that week that they'd drank, Anna wasn't going to let herself feel guilty. Normally, they were both incredibly conservative with alcohol, but life had been so stressful that it was a welcome release after all they'd endured. She wasn't going to make it a habit. They needed to keep their health and wits about them if they were going to survive the next few weeks of construction and chaos. Looking at the empty built-in bookshelf that stood across the sitting room from an ancient fireplace, she smiled and dreamed of filling it up with the famous authors who had guided her through life.

Had it not been for the fictional worlds created between the pages, Anna knew she'd have never made it out of the foster system with her sanity intact. They'd been an escape for her until she'd found her footing and passions as an adult. Now, knowing she might be able to one day have that same impact on others, Anna was excited to get started on the renovations so they could open the doors to the public. Looking around the room, she caught Emily's gaze once more and smiled as she shook her head.

"It's unreal, right?" Anna said.

Emily nodded. "You can say that again. I know we're here, and I can see that it's real, but my head's in a fog over it. I don't know where to start."

"Plus, the followers…"

Her friend gave a low whistle and nodded in silent agreement. They'd gained several hundred thousand followers since starting the process of renovating the estate, and the money, though nothing record-breaking, was slowly growing to be just enough to not only cover the tab they had with Peter but start on the next round of renovations as well. With the plumbing next on the roster and the electricity up and running, it was time for the women to get to work. Though neither was afraid of a challenge, it would be an interesting feat, nonetheless.

She couldn't wait to show the townsfolk, especially those with attitudes like Nancy's, that they had what it took to make the estate shine again. They were both determined to bring life back to the mansion and the surrounding area. Anna had to believe that sooner or later, the locals would see that they were trying to help and not hinder by keeping things small, quaint, and quiet. Until then, they would keep using their platform to generate buzz about the new business. It was the only way they could bring the house back from the dead.

"What are we going to do with the furniture that's left behind?" Emily asked. "I bet some of it can be saved or restored by Lori."

"Then let's get her up here and give her first dibs on it. If we can keep the original pieces, that would be ideal. I know it's going to cost a little more to bring them back to life, but I think it's the right thing to do. What do you think?" Anna asked.

"I agree. We'll find a way to make it work. If the

ghost of Claymont Harrington is floating around here, I don't want to be pissing him off by getting rid of all his stuff."

She chuckled. "I hope he's not here, but it would make sense. A man that angry at his family is bound to have a few lingering issues tying him to the ground."

"Do you think we should try to track them down? The relatives, I mean. You never know. Maybe they aren't that bad anymore. It's been years, after all."

"I don't know about all that. Maybe once we've got this place restored and have completed everything we want done, we could look into it, but until then, I think we've got our hands full just trying to bring it back to life. We can leave the dead and live for another day, if you ask me."

"Agreed," Emily said. "I just know this place is going to be a hit. Who could not love it?"

"I don't know. It's amazing if you ask me, but some people out there just want to start trouble. Once we've established a residence here and made it our own, we can look into the family history."

"You know my father would never let anyone take this from us, but I get what you're saying. No reason to go poking any wasps' nests."

Anna's jaw dropped.

"What?" Emily muttered.

"Nothing...it's just...I don't think I've ever heard

you back down from the idea of starting a shit-storm. It's unexpected, is all," Anna said.

Emily burst into laughter. "Believe it or not, I can pretend to be a grown-up every once in a while. It's not something I like to do, but hey, if keeping my mouth shut will get us to the finish line at this place faster, that's what I'll do."

"Well, I'm proud of you nonetheless, and I appreciate the gesture. Don't worry. When the time comes, I'll give you the honor of shouting it from the rooftop," Anna said.

"That's if the roof will hold me."

"Ha! Don't worry, that's on the list of things to repair, too."

They enjoyed their success for a little while longer while topping off their glasses. When the champagne was gone, the pair made their way out to the van and started packing up their belongings. Though they stayed in cabins and bungalows, yurts, and tents sporadically, depending on where their travels took them, it was the first time they'd be cleaning out the van and camper to put down roots. She was looking forward to the change of pace and getting into the camper combo to do a good deep clean when time permitted. With everything they had going on, though, Anna knew it wouldn't happen for several weeks yet.

Together for several hours, they worked, hauling and packing, doing light housework as they offloaded their possessions into the new home. At long last, after what felt like an eternity, the task was done, and they were both exhausted. It was nearly eleven by the time she crawled into her bed for the first time. The queen-sized mattress was new, along with the frame in both rooms. It felt good knowing she could doze off into a restful sleep.

29

"Are you sure you're okay? I don't think I've ever seen you not finish your bacon," Emily said.

Anna nodded, doing her best to smile as she forced another piece down her throat. It was going to be an incredibly long day if Emily kept asking her if she was okay. Her friend was just concerned about her exhausted appearance, but Anna didn't want to add to Emily's burden. The night hadn't gone as planned. Instead of sleeping restfully in her new bed, she had been woken up every few hours by the most horrific and vivid dreams she'd ever encountered. Not only had they left her shaken, but they'd made Anna question if moving into the mansion was a mistake altogether.

"I'm fine, I promise. Just those new-bed jitters," Anna said.

Emily pursed her lips. "Odd, since that's never happened to you before. Are you sure that's all it is?"

"Yes, now let's drop it and get on to something worth talking about. This view sure is something, huh? It's going to be a huge selling point for the bed and breakfast."

"You've got that right," Emily said.

Looking out over the back lawn of the estate, she was glad that Emily had dropped the topic of her night. Even as she replayed the dreams in her head, it seemed like the rantings of an insane person. They had found the back patio in surprisingly good condition while hunting for an ideal breakfast location. Given how accustomed they were to having breakfast outside, it seemed like the obvious choice. Something had drawn her through the kitchen doors and out to the back of the estate that morning, and now she was incredibly thankful she had. The property continued to surprise her. Before long, the pair finished their breakfast and headed back into the estate to start working.

The construction crew had started to arrive for the major repairs while they started stripping away wallpaper from the sections that had been cleared. Though the work was tedious, it was made lighter with Emily at her side. Every so often, Anna would snap pictures of their progress and upload them onto the website and social media platforms. In doing so, they were boosting their views and, hopefully, their income. Bit by bit, the home was starting to come to life again. She knew by the time they opened their doors to the public, it would be something majestic to behold. With the windows opened and a slight breeze moving through, they sang and danced while working to the radio the contractors had playing outside.

After debating over it for a solid twenty minutes, the pair were working on moving a small sofa out to the waiting dumpster now parked in the driveway. Anna had wanted to try to save it, sending it to Lori for refurbishing, but a cursory inspection had revealed not only a family of rodents living within its confines but also an unhealthy number of termites. Given that the house had thus far proven pest-free, it wasn't worth the gamble of allowing the piece to stay inside. Just as they heaved it over the edge, she heard a car pulling up the blacktop driveway and turned, her stomach clenching with recognition.

Nancy climbed out of the parked car, a smirk on her lips and a manila folder in her hand. Right away, Anna felt Emily tense next to her and wondered what new battlefront they were going to be faced with. It made no sense that the woman seemed to have it out for them when all they'd done was win the lottery that she'd listed along with the other locals. More and more, it felt like they were being punished for that, and it made no sense. She wasn't going to let Nancy bring them down. Whatever she wanted to throw at them next, they would be ready for it.

"Nancy...what a surprise," Emily muttered.

"Good morning, ladies. It's nice to see that you're working on this old place. I was starting to wonder if letting you stay here was going to be a mistake," she said.

"*Letting us stay*? Last time I checked, the deed was in Anna's name, so there is no 'letting us' about it, lady," Emily growled.

Nancy pursed her lips, somehow appearing shocked by the way Emily spoke to her after the way she'd been treating them. Without a word, Nancy handed Anna the folder and turned her attention away from Emily. It was a deliberate move on the mayor's part without question to make Emily feel like she wasn't a part of the conversation. Anna didn't care what the property deed said; they were working on the restoration project together despite only Anna's name being on the formal forms. She wanted to smack the smug look right from the woman's face but knew it would only cause them more problems.

"What is this?" Anna asked.

"Well, after seeing how things are going and your general disregard for the rules of our community—"

"Excuse me?" Emily snarled.

"Oh, don't play coy. Pulling up, I saw that you haven't managed to get tags on that old piece of crap by the garage. I did a little digging on you, missy, but it turns out you don't care all that much about any rules. It seems you've got something of a lead foot?"

"Are you kidding me?" Emily snapped. "You looked up my driving record? You have lost your mind, lady."

"My name is Nancy, *girl*," Nancy barked.

Anna could see that a fight was coming if she didn't step in. Clearing her throat, she placed herself between Nancy and Emily before redirecting the conversation back to the folder. Ignoring the glares of them both, she opened it and found an official document from the town magistrate. As she read through it, Anna felt her cheeks flushing with rage as her gaze darted back to Nancy. Now, she felt like the one who needed holding back.

"You're taxing us?" she stammered.

"Oh, now we could never tax one particular business, honey. No, we held a special council last night to decide on what the best course would be for our community going forward. In light of all the big new plans the two of you have, we decided it would best serve the town if we placed an added local tax on larger corporations."

Emily snatched the document from Anna's hand, scanning it over before chuckling and shoving it back into the envelope. "This is for any business over twenty-five hundred square feet. Tell me, Nancy, how many businesses meet that criteria in this town? Huh?" Emily asked.

"Well, right now, there is just one, but I'm sure

there will be more. Why, we would never target you…"

All the anger and pent-up rage she'd been feeling toward the woman was boiling to the top. Anna could feel her hands trembling slightly, the emotions surging through her without anything to stop them from coming out.

"Leave," Anna growled.

The smirk fell from Nancy's lips. "Excuse me?"

"I said get the fuck off my property, and the next time you set foot here, I'll have you arrested," Anna said.

Nancy gasped, taking a step back. "Young lady—"

"Leave!" Anna screamed.

The woman jumped, now appearing both shocked and terrified, as she raced away from them and jumped into her car. Anna could see the look of pure fury on Nancy's expression as she peeled away. Taking several deep breaths to calm herself back down, Anna turned to Emily, who looked just as stunned as Nancy had, but there was a smile on her face, a shocked pride evident in her expression.

"Whoa, who are you, and what have you done with Anna? Jesus, I don't think I've ever heard you scream like that *or* throw around the F-bomb."

"Thirty percent, Emily. They want us to pay an additional business tax of thirty freaking percent. That's insane!"

"Yeah, well, she can try to push through whatever

she wants because Nancy and the town council don't have what we do, my father."

"Do you think he's going to be able to help us out? I feel like we should reconsider selling the—"

"Don't you dare say it," Emily said. "We are not selling the Impala. Come on, let's grab a cup of coffee and give him a call."

Anna nodded and followed Emily, but the anger she felt deep inside wouldn't subside. Nancy was out for blood, and Anna was determined to figure out why. She wasn't sure how many more hits they could take before things became too much for them and their finances to handle. Stepping over the home's threshold, though, Anna knew what they were fighting for. They wouldn't be bullied, and they weren't going to give up, no matter what Nancy tried to pull.

30

"How long have you girls had your LLC?" Russ asked.

Anna looked at Emily, who shrugged. They had been on the call for nearly twenty minutes, and in that time, the man had managed to ease both of their minds. The rest of the time had been spent answering sporadic questions before Emily's father inevitably stuck them on hold again to confer with the rest of the lawyers at his firm. As much as she appreciated everything they were doing for the friends, the guilt over knowing what they normally made an hour was starting to weigh on her.

"A little over two years," Anna said. "I can get you the exact date if you want. I just need to get on the state site and—"

"Nope, two years is good. Are you sure it was over two years, though?"

"Yeah, Pops. We even have a little celebration when we hit that mark what…like three months ago?" Emily said.

"That sounds about right," Anna said.

"Perfect, I'll be right back," Russ said.

As the call was once more placed on hold, Anna looked at her friend, but Emily simply shrugged. She didn't know any more about the legalities than Anna did. It was infuriating to her that they were once more counting on Russ to figure out the tight situation they were in. She hated that he was always the first person they called, but she knew he was happy to help the pair. Emily's family was downright amazing, and she considered them her own, knowing they felt the same way about her. Watching Emily tapping her fingers on the countertop of the van, she smiled and shook her head.

"I'm starting to think we need to keep your dad on retainer."

Emily snorted. "As if we could afford that. The Impala *might* cover a few hours, but then we'd be sitting ducks again."

"I guess it's a good thing he likes us then," she muttered.

"He loves us, and you know it. He would do anything to help us out. Hell, I had to talk him out of flying here with Mom just to fund the project and smack everyone into line, like Nancy and—"

The phone clicked as Russ came back on the line.

"Girls? We've got some good news for you. I didn't want to say anything earlier until I was sure, but Kenny over here just got off the line with Judge Townsend. Do you guys remember her?"

"Yeah, she's retired now, right?" Anna said.

"That's right. She took a job after retiring, though, with a local tax firm that works hand in hand with the Federal Department of Taxation. She reached out to a few people she knows on her end to confirm."

"Love the background info, Pops, but the suspense is killing us over here," Emily said.

Russ chuckled. "All right, so basically, since you've already been an established LLC in California and your business is listed as a traveling one, the house is going to fall under that same listing until it's time to update your address once you're settled. Now, you'll have to pay the taxes here of twelve percent, but as long as you keep your LLC in good standing in the state of California, you can list the estate under it as well, and it will only be taxed once by the state. Now, this Nancy woman can appeal that, but it's going to take her a long time and get the village tied up in a lot of legal fees."

"So, we aren't out thirty percent?" Anna asked.

"Nope, just keep doing what you've been doing, and I'll double-check your books tonight when I get home, but the last time I looked them over when you filed a few months ago, everything looked just like it should."

Both women let out a sigh of relief. It was hard to believe that they'd been so worked up over the situation. Moreover, it was going to feel damn good when Nancy realized they didn't have to pay. With that in mind, Anna knew they needed to start playing hardball with the woman. As Emily wrapped up the call with her father, Anna grabbed her laptop and started sending an email to Nancy and the village council.

"I think that any communications with these guys should go through me from now on," Russ said. "Or at least carbon copy me in them and forward any questions pertaining to the tax status to me."

"You've got it," Anna said. "I was just about to email her and let her know what you said so that works out perfectly. Honestly, I don't want to deal with her any more than I have, too."

"Then your wish is my command, kiddo. Copy me on the email and let her know I'll be handling it from here. If she tries to reach out, just ignore her. I'll officially list myself as your representation for all legal matters."

"Russ, we can't thank you enough," Anna said.

"Don't mention it. We are all just so proud of the two of you and how far you've come. Emily, you found your own path, and Anna, you overcame a childhood that not many can. We are here for anything you guys need. Don't worry about the mayor; focus on making that place your home. I'll deal with her."

As the call came to an end and Anna finished writing the email, she sent it after adding the town council to the email along with Russ's firm. Though he had a personal email address, she used the one at the law office to add an extra layer of pomp to the recipients. If they wanted to start a war, the friends would give them one with an entire army behind them. Before she had time to close her computer, Anna's phone started to ring. Seeing Nancy's name appear on the screen, she grinned and sent the call to voicemail.

"Whoa, that was fast. Something tells me they didn't like your response," Emily said.

Anna chuckled. "Yeah, well, I don't like feeling threatened in my own home. We won the auction for the house. We are on the deed, and I'm not going to be bullied by her. She asked for this when she started it."

"You go, girl. Trust me, I'm pumped to see you so worked up over it. It's about time if you ask me. That woman had a burr up her butt from day one."

Anna rolled her eyes but knew Emily was right. From the moment the mayor had learned they were going to restore the house and not tear it down or sell it off again, she had been giving them a hard time. With each new attempt that the town council made to close down their operations, Anna found herself more determined to put down roots and dig in her heels.

"Well, that's not how I saw our afternoon going, but I'm happy that we've got your dad on our side. He's amazing for doing all this," she said.

Emily chuckled. "Are you joking? He loves getting to jump in and help us. I think he misses the days when we had to call him for gas money."

"Do you remember being in Wisconsin our first time when the heater went out? I thought we were going to freeze to death."

Emily nodded. "Then Dad showed up, his designer jacket all covered in dust from the tow-truck driver's seats. He was so worried, he almost took a sabbatical from work right then and there to try to get us to come home."

"Or travel with us. Don't forget that one. Your mom had an RV picked out and everything to follow us around the country. They're pretty amazing people."

"That's the truth, so what do you say we go make them proud and get this beast up and running? God knows I'd love to see us turning a profit before the end of the year."

"And that might actually be possible since we won't be paying those ridiculous taxes," Anna said.

"Don't get me started on that again. I'm just angry enough to answer the next time she calls and give her a piece of my mind. She's becoming a real pain in our asses."

"Yeah, trust me, I know how you feel."

"I suppose we should let Pops handle it, though. That's the 'adult' thing to do…even if it's a lot less fun. Just once, I'd like to tell her where she can shove her bad attitude," Emily said.

Anna nodded and grabbed her phone at the same time it rang. Once more, seeing Nancy's name on the screen, she sent it to voicemail and slipped the phone into her pocket as they headed out the van's doors. Nothing was going to stop them from making their dreams come true, not as long as they had a fighting chance and Emily's parents on their side.

31

"You look perfect, I promise," Anna said.

Emily smiled at her. "Thanks, I just hope Lori doesn't think it's too over the top. I can't remember the last time I wore a skirt."

"Well, you're pulling it off. You had better get going, though, or you're going to be late picking her up. I don't think she'd like that very much."

Emily nodded and looked at herself once more in the shared bathroom mirror before giving Anna a hug and heading out Anna's bedroom door. Watching her friend go, Anna couldn't help but smile, knowing Emily and Lori were going to have an amazing evening together. It was their first official date, and they'd been looking forward to it for some time. Making her way to the new sofa in her sitting room, Anna grabbed one of her favorite fiction off the shelf and opened it to the last place she'd started reading. It was wonderful to be getting into some semblance of a routine. Anna didn't know how long she had been sitting there when a strange noise in the hallway made her pause.

At first, she was certain Emily was returning from her date. Happy that she'd made it back home, Anna stood and stretched out, making her way to the bedroom door to greet Emily. It was strange how the evening heat had settled inside the old estate. The muggy air felt thick around her. Not quite awake and tired, Anna yawned and tugged open the door. Gazing out into the dim hallway, she frowned. Emily was nowhere in sight. It had taken her a minute to get off the sofa, and it was possible that her friend had already retreated into her room.

Anna stepped out into the hallway, her body naturally turning to head for Emily's room, when a noise down the other way grabbed her attention. Given it was a construction zone, there was no reason for Emily to be in the area. She wouldn't take any risks showing Lori around so late at night. Her heart had started to race in a manner that made Anna uneasy. There was something strange about the way the night felt, a darkness that seemed to be lingering deep in her soul. She couldn't place the strange sensation but knew it was nothing good.

"Emily? Lori? Did you guys make it back?" she called out.

Met with only silence, Anna swallowed despite

how dry her throat felt. She didn't know what to make of the situation and hoped it wasn't some cruel jump-scare from her friend. Faced with that, though, or the alternative, an intruder in their home, she'd take Emily's antics and shenanigans. She let out a weighted sigh and forced herself to continue on down the hall. Moving from the main section to the right wing that ran the length of the west side of the mansion, her stomach tightened.

Save for a few dim lights, the hall was dark and foreboding. She had nearly convinced herself that there was nothing but a few wayward mice when once more Anna heard the noise. The strange rustling was easy to pinpoint once her body and sight had adjusted to the dim lighting. She squinted nonetheless, her gaze focusing on a large side buffet sitting beneath the front windows of the mansion. It was easily six feet long and three feet wide, towering a good four feet off the ground. The solid wood piece was one they'd intended to restore and keep in its place. Peter had explained to them that removing it would not only be costly, but the piece would need to be dismantled to make that happen.

After consulting with Lori and the woman, who gladly took on the restoration task in-house, she was happy they'd opted to keep it. It was a beautiful talking point, but now, she worried a family of rodents or even larger vermin was trying to call it home as well. When Anna was five feet from the buffet, she paused. The sound of rustling once more reached her ears as her heart pounded. It was one thing to be brave when it was her against a handful of mice, but anything bigger would make Anna's confidence waver. Though she didn't particularly mind raccoons, opossums, and the like, she also didn't want to come face-to-face with them alone in the middle of the night. A brief moment of hesitation made her pause.

"Listen, guys, if you just go find somewhere else to crash for the night, no one needs to get hurt..."

She was met with a tense silence that hung heavy in the air. Suddenly, the noise that had seemed so faint at first burst through the quiet of the night just as a figure emerged from behind the wooden piece. Anna screamed, jumping backward as the man raced down the hall past her. It was as though he didn't see her as his face contorted into an expression of fear. He moved within inches of her, a pungent and foul smell following him as he sprinted toward the front doors. For a split second, she was frozen with fear before her instinct took over, and she gave chase.

"Hey!" Anna yelled. "Stop!"

The man didn't listen as he skidded to a stop by the front doors. Though he reached for them and they were unlocked, it seemed as if he were trapped in the house. As she approached, he turned, his eyes filled with fear as they gazed at something beyond her. She spun around to see what had caused him such fear but found nothing. Turning back, Anna gasped. The man's face was changing, distorting as the skin slumped, sliding down into unnatural shapes before breaking free from his scalp and slipping off. She stumbled backward, the stench and horror consuming her as she tried to scream, but nothing came out. The now-ghastly figure with exposed bones took a step toward her, as if he were seeing her for the first time.

"Help me," he whispered.

Blood gurgled from his lips as he spoke, his teeth falling onto the floor between them. Anna screamed once more; this time, the noise filled the air. She squeezed her eyes closed, and the world around her started to spin.

"Anna!" Emily yelled.

Her eyes shot open, the panic fresh in her mind as she scrambled away from her friend's touch, climbing over the back of the sofa and frantically looking around. The room was cool, and the air was crisp. The soft glow of the television she'd left playing in the background while reading now rambling on about whatever the late-night infomercial was trying to sell. Suddenly, she was aware of someone else in the room with them, and she spun around to see Lori standing in the bathroom doorway that connected the two rooms. She looked just as shocked as Emily.

"Hey, take it easy, Anna. It's just us…what happened? Are you okay?"

At that moment, Anna realized the whole thing had been a dream. Even as it dawned on her, though, it wasn't just a bad nightmare but something deeper and darker. Her cheeks flushed with embarrassment, nonetheless.

"I'm sorry. It was just a nightmare. I guess I dozed off," she muttered.

"Don't apologize. They happen to us all," Lori said. "You just scared us. We were worried something terrible had happened in here."

She cringed, not having the heart to tell the woman she was certain something horrible had, in fact, happened at the estate, and now, Anna was being forced to watch it repeatedly in her sleep. Instead, she simply shook her head and forced herself to smile, hoping it would put them both at ease.

"I'm fine. I promise. I should probably try sleeping in my bed. You two go and enjoy your evening. Sorry again for the disruption," Anna said.

Lori nodded and headed back to Emily's room, but her friend didn't budge. She could feel the woman's intense gaze on her, poking at the façade that she'd created to put their minds at ease. Anna sighed and rolled her eyes, giving her friend a grin.

"I'm fine. It looks like things are going well with you two, so you better get back to it," Anna said.

"Are you sure? Yeah, we are having a good time, but if you need me to send her home and hang out—"

"I don't, Emily. I promise it was just a bad dream. Now go before she starts to think you don't like her."

Emily grinned and finally headed back through the bathroom to her own room. When both the doors were closed, Anna let out the breath she'd been holding, her body trembling with fear. Collapsing onto the sofa once more, she knew there would be no more sleep for her. The dead had made sure of that.

32

The bitter taste of her coffee did little to help Anna wake up. Instead, all it was doing was making her hands shake more as she looked out the sitting room window. Though she had tried to sleep a few times after the harrowing nightmare, it was impossible for her mind to allow her to rest. She was terrified of having the dream again. Everything about it had seemed so real at the time. There were moments when she was nearly certain she could smell the lingering stench of decay in the hallway but hoped it was just her mind playing tricks on her. Anna knew Emily was worried about her. Their paths had crossed again that morning when she'd been making coffee in the kitchen. Though it had been almost six, she hadn't expected Emily to be up for several more hours.

After convincing her friend once more that she

was fine, Emily left Anna alone and returned to bed. Now, as the clock moved slowly toward eight when the contractors would start arriving and working for the day, Anna was filled with dread. She didn't know that she wanted to be surrounded by noise and people for the next several hours, but she couldn't ask them to take the day off simply because she wasn't feeling up to it. Instead, she had every intention of taking off in the Impala and heading out for a drive once the crew arrived and started work. Anna sipped on her now-cold coffee, once more letting her mind travel back to the nightmare until the sound of approaching feet pulled her back out.

When she looked up and saw Lori, two fresh cups of the steaming brew in her hands, Anna smiled. She wasn't about to pry but knew Lori hadn't just pulled up to visit with them. The woman had spent the night and, from the looks of things, seemed incredibly happy with the outcome. She handed Anna a cup and sat in the chair across from her. For a moment, neither of them spoke, and Anna was happy to find that Lori was comfortable sitting in silence, but as she took the first sip of her fresh cup, all of that changed. She groaned with pleasure.

"Thanks," Anna said. "I think I've been sipping the same cold cup for the last hour."

"You're welcome. I thought you could use a refresher when I saw you here earlier. I hope it's okay that I'm joining you. If you want, though, I can find somewhere else—"

"No, no, no, you're fine. Honestly, I'm tired of having conversations with myself in my head anyway. I hope you're not waiting for Emily to wake up on her own. That woman would sleep all day if she could."

Lori chuckled. "Don't worry, I think she set an alarm. I don't have much going on today, and normally, the shop's closed, so I thought I'd see if there was anything I could help you out with around here."

"Yes, that would be awesome. We could definitely use someone with your experience and knowledge. I just don't want to be taking you away from your actual job. I know how hard it is to run a small business and stay afloat."

Lori hesitated. "It's okay. Today is my day off anyway. Plus, you seemed pretty freaked out last night, and I can only presume that the stress of this place has something to do with that. I don't want to see you get burned out and call it quits."

"I appreciate that," Anna said.

She let out a heavy sigh as the woman watched her. For the first time, Anna felt like she could share what had happened the night before in her dream. They might not have known each other for long, but Anna knew Lori would understand. She had already voiced her belief in the supernatural before then to Emily, a detail she had shared with Anna not long after. If there was any chance that Lori might be able to help her sort out the terrifying nightmares, she had to take the risk of sounding crazed. When she finished, Anna was happy to see that Lori wasn't calling the paramedics to have her locked up or running for the door.

"Honestly, if I'd have known all that last night, we'd have all three gone back to my place," Lori said. "I live in an apartment above the shop, but the guest room is always open for you."

"Thanks, I appreciate that, but I don't think I'd have left. It's just not who I am. I'm not going to let a few bad dreams scare me away from this place. It's our home now. Sooner or later, my messed-up head will come to terms with that."

"I wouldn't be so hard on yourself. This place has some powerful energies. Hell, I could feel them the first time I saw it, and walking into it?" She gave a low whistle. "The whole place is damn near vibrating. You can't turn a corner without feeling like someone's watching your every move."

Anna let out a sigh of relief. "Oh, thank God. I was starting to think it was just me!"

"Not at all. I'm just sorry we didn't talk about it sooner. I think we should look more into your dream. Who knows, it might mean something."

"Listen, I'll try anything if you think it might help. I can't keep surviving on cold coffee and no sleep. If I wasn't crazy before, it would definitely push me over the edge."

"Do you think you could describe this man for me?" Lori asked. "I know that might sound like a strange request, but I have a theory about it if you'll just hear me out."

Anna was thrilled that her new friend wasn't bolting for the hills and complied with Lori's request. It made her stomach lurch at the memory of the man's dark eyes and hair, his gaunt figure, and the outdated suit he wore. More than anything, though, it was the smell that continued to assault her. It wasn't lingering in the air—it had never been there to start with—but her mind insisted on circling back to it at every opportunity.

When she was done giving the description, Anna saw that the color had drained from Lori's cheeks. She was sitting in silence, seemingly lost in a daze. At that moment, she wondered if the description had been too much, if it was the straw that would break the camel's back, and Lori was finally going to run from home, screaming about Anna's insanity. Instead, she snapped out of the trance and reached into her pocket, grabbing her phone and ignoring Anna completely. Stunned, Anna didn't know what to make of the woman's bizarre reaction and watched her for several seconds.

Just as quickly as Lori had grabbed her phone and begun ignoring Anna, her attention snapped back to her. She turned her phone around, and Anna gasped. Staring back at her in a photo that had been taken long before her time was the man from the horrible dream the night before. As a chill ran down her spine, she reached out and took the phone, looking at the man in closer detail. She wondered if it was all in her head or if her mind was distorting the photo to make the chaos seem less. Handing it back to Lori, though, Anna knew the truth. The man was the same. The only difference was the state of his body. In the photo, he was alive and well, but in her dream, his eyes had been cold and dead.

"I don't understand," Anna stammered. "That's the man from my dream. How is that possible?"

Lori set down her phone. "Anna, I don't think it was a dream at all. You said he looked through you as if you weren't there, right?"

"Right," she said.

"That's because you weren't there, at least not the first time it happened. I think something else is going on here. That man died here over twenty years ago…"

"What? That's not possible. How could I be dreaming about someone I've never seen before? I have not done any digging into this place with regard to the people who died here yet. I know I never saw that man before last night."

"There is something more happening here, Anna. I think someone is trying to reach you from the other side."

As the words settled around her, Anna felt like she was going to be sick. It didn't make any sense, and yet, all the puzzle pieces fit together. Gazing once more at the phone sitting on the table, Anna felt the now-familiar chill of someone watching her running down her spine. For the first time, though, she realized it wasn't all in her head. There had been someone watching her every move. Or rather *something.*

33

"Who is he?" she asked, her voice barely whispering.

"His name was Ryan Snyder—"

Her head snapped up. "Snyder?"

Lori nodded. "Yeah, that's right, our town's esteemed financial advisor, Janice Snyder, is his widow. They said it was a hunting accident, but not many folks around here believe that. Janice didn't report him missing for three days, and by the time they pulled his body out of the creek…"

"His skin was falling off," she whispered.

"Yeah."

"How in the hell didn't we know about this? That woman has been after us since day one and come to find out, she might have killed her husband here? Why here?"

Lori shrugged. "Some people think she was just following in her sister's footsteps."

Anna groaned, already knowing the story was about to get ten times worse. She wasn't sure she wanted to hear any more of the lore after discovering that the man she'd dreamed about had likely been murdered there years before. For a moment, she thought she was going to get sick to her stomach, but she was quick to recover. They had to keep pressing forward. If she was going to unravel what was happening at the estate, then not getting answers would be a terrible idea, no matter how bad things got. Anna only wished that Emily was awake to hear everything, too. Her friend would love the haunting tale.

"Jesus, her sister killed someone here, too? Maybe I'm starting to understand why they had such a hard time getting rid of this place. At the very least, we need to invest in a taller fence," she muttered.

Lori chuckled. "Oh, you know her sister pretty well, too. From what Emily's told me, she'd been giving you one hell of a time."

Suddenly, her mind made the connection, and she groaned once more. Almost every time they'd encountered Janice, the mayor had been at her side or giving her orders from her office. Anna couldn't believe she hadn't noticed how similar the woman's features were looking back on things. Normally, she was incredibly good at spotting the same facial structure, build, and traits when it came to family relations.

"My God, it's the mayor, isn't it?" Anna asked.

"Yep, and she happens to be a widow as well," Lori said. "Her husband passed a few weeks before Ryan did. The police report said it was an accident, that Neil Thomas 'fell' down the main staircase while looking the place over with his wife."

"And people actually bought into that?"

She shrugged. "Around here, those women have always carried weight, at least as long as I have been here. It's a benefit of being Claymont Harrington's granddaughters. People might not like them, but they don't go against them, either, especially not after their husbands both up and died."

"Jesus God almighty. It's no wonder they wanted to get rid of this place, and now they want us gone. I bet there is evidence or something here tying them to it. Now I'm having dreams about dead men, too?" Anna said.

Shaking her head, she struggled to keep the world around her from spinning. Anna was already on the edge of exhaustion, and now that the picture was becoming clear, she didn't know if she was up for the fight. It was one thing to go against the two women behind the legal shield Russ had provided, but they were fighting on an entirely different level. No home was worth dying for, not even the Harrington estate. At that moment, Anna no longer knew what to do and needed to talk with Emily. As if her friend knew she was needed, the study door opened, and Emily, clutching a cup of coffee and barely looking awake, came in and sat down.

"What's up?" Emily mumbled.

"Oh man, you aren't going to believe this…" Anna said.

As she started going through everything she had just learned, weaving in detail about her dream in the mix, she watched her friend become alert. It was hard to process it all; she knew that much firsthand, but Emily had a temper. Her cheeks flushed when the connection between the property and the mayor, along with her sister, was reviled. She saw the mystery of it all, along with the intrigue by the home's obvious haunting, but more than anything else, Emily saw the cold-hearted approach that the sisters had taken not only to their husbands and the townspeople but to the friends sitting there as well. That alone was enough to make her see red.

"Those bitches," she snarled. "They aren't going to get away with this. I've got half a mind to go tell them what I think right now."

"Take it easy, honey," Lori said. "We already know they aren't afraid of getting their hands dirty. I would hate to lose you before getting to know you."

Emily softened, a detail that shocked Anna but made her heart soar at the same time. Though the young couple couldn't see it yet, Anna knew they were soulmates and destined to be together. She wouldn't let her friend put that all on the line just to blow off some steam. Nothing was more important than their lives.

"I think we need to take a minute here and cool down. Maybe we should talk about getting a hotel room for a couple of days or taking the van to a campground," Anna said.

"You mean turn tail and run? Give them a chance to torch this place? Is there any proof that might be hiding here? Hell no. I'm not going anywhere," Emily growled.

"I have to agree with her," Lori said. "If you guys leave now, it will only strengthen their grip on this place and the town. At least here, you can do something to protect yourselves. Plus, we might be able to get help on finding the proof we need."

"Oh yeah? How?" Anna asked.

"Well, it's a little unorthodox, so you'll have to bear with me here. How would you feel about bringing in a medium?"

"You mean like a 'talks to the dead' kind of medium?" Emily asked.

Lori nodded. "Like I said, it's a little out there, but only four people know what happened on the nights that those two men died, and two of them are dead. I don't think we'll be getting a confession from Nancy or Janice anytime soon."

"So, talking to the men might be the only way," Anna said.

She looked at Emily, trying to process the proposition, and read her friend at the same time. Lori hadn't been joking about it being a wild idea, but given everything Anna had felt and seen in the last few days, she was willing to try anything. Something at the estate was trying to communicate with them. They wouldn't know until they reached out if that entity was there to help or hinder their progress. Her stomach lurched at the idea of seeing the dead man again, but they had no choice. Their home wasn't safe for them. Not from the dead or the living.

"All right, you've got my vote," Anna said. "What do you think, Emily? We won't move forward without your approval, too. This isn't just my home."

"Yeah, well, it's not just mine, either. From the sound of things, we aren't alone, and that definitely doesn't sit right with me. If reaching out to this… spirit is the way to get our home back, then I'm on board. I just want to see those witches down at Town Hall get what they've got coming."

Despite the windows all being closed, a breeze suddenly moved through the room. For a moment, she thought it was in her head until she looked at the others and saw they, too, had felt it. It was the first time that confirmation had come that they were on the right path, but she didn't know if it was a good thing or a bad one. Either way, they were going to find out.

"Something tells me you aren't the only one who wants those two to answer for what they've done," Anna said.

Emily pursed her lips, moving closer to Lori and wrapping her arm protectively around the woman. It was a touching sight to witness, but she hated that Emily no longer felt safe in their home. They had worked so hard to get the estate and keep it. Now, unsure if they were even wanted there, she couldn't help but wonder once more if they were making the right decision. Part of her wanted to leave the house and never come back. From the other side of the room, Anna and the others watched as the door leading out to the hall slowly started to close on its own.

Anna swallowed. "Either that, or they don't like us poking around in the past. Let's hope whatever that thing is, it's on our side."

34

Not long after the conversation wrapped up, she felt a little down about the situation. Anna didn't know if it was the house or if it was simply the lack of sleep, but she needed some space to clear her head. Emily, though it seemed, wasn't on board with her being anywhere out of sight. It was strange to see the woman in such a protective role. Anna adored Emily for wanting to watch over her and keep her safe, but it was starting to feel a little suffocating. As she sat on the sofa to put on her shoes, Emily sat next to her and smiled.

"I think I hear Peter and his crew pulling in. Are you going to see where they're starting for the day?" Emily asked.

"That was the idea. After that, I think I will take the Impala out for a cruise. I could use some time behind the wheel," Anna said.

"An afternoon cruise? That sounds like heaven to me. Let me get my shoes, and we can take off," Emily said.

"Actually, one of us needs to stay here in case Peter or his crew have any questions. I know they are just about finished with the roof. I don't want to slow them down by having to wait on us for answers."

"That's why they invented phones. What's wrong?"

"Nothing, I was just sort of hoping for some time alone. I don't want to upset you or anything. I just need some fresh air."

"Are you sure? You didn't get any sleep last night. I don't think being behind the wheel is the best idea."

"I appreciate that you are worried about me, but I am a big girl. Please, Emily. Just stay here and keep an eye on things for me."

Though she could see that her friend wasn't thrilled at the idea of being left behind or, more so, letting Anna go off on her own, Emily nodded in agreement. It was hard for her to disappoint Emily. But so much had happened, and they'd uncovered such a huge secret that she needed time on her own not only to think but to plan their next move as well. She had to believe there was a way to bring peace to the spirits and to bring the sister to justice as well. That wasn't going to happen unless she could come up with a plan. After getting her shoes tied, she grabbed the keys to the Impala hanging on her bedroom wall and turned back once more to smile at Emily.

"I promise I'll be back within the hour, okay? I'm not going to go far. I'm just hoping that the open road clears my head some. I didn't sleep much last night, but I'm not going to be daydreaming behind the wheel, either."

"You say that now, but once that warm sun hits you, you never know what might happen."

"Have a little faith in me. I'll pull over and give you a call if I get sleepy. Deal?"

"Deal, but you promise you'll call? You won't try to tough it out?" Emily asked.

Anna nodded and turned for the bedroom door. By the time she was pulling the Impala out of the garage, the workers were going at the siding and windows with full force. She gave Emily and Peter a wave as she rolled down the driveway and turned right. The winding country road would take her away from the house and the village, through the forest and across the hills. It was just what she needed. The road rolled out in front of her, the sloping hills and dipping valleys making her stomach rise and fall with butterflies each time. Despite her confidence behind the wheel of the Impala, she kept her speed reasonable.

A cruise was meant to be enjoyed, not barreled through at seventy miles per hour. As she crested the top of one particularly steep hill, she marveled at the view of the plowed fields below. It was the sort of thing Emily would love to see. Knowing she had to snap a picture for her friend, she pressed the brake to pull the car over onto the gravel shoulder. When nothing happened, Anna's heart started to race. She pushed down on the pedal again, this time with more force, but it went straight to the floor. Watching the speedometer climbing as the downhill slope whipped her speeds faster and faster, Anna grabbed the emergency brake and slowly started pulling it up.

Just as the Impala reached eighty, she felt the emergency brake catch and the car started to slow. It was hard to control the roving beast with one hand while feathering the brake with the other. With her heart pounding and her chest heaving, Anna finally managed to bring the car to a stop at the bottom of the hill, rolling it into the gravel and slipping it into park before killing the engine. She felt like she was going to be sick as she jumped out from behind the wheel, grabbing her phone at the last minute and stumbling away in shock. Immediately, she dialed Emily's number. She answered on the first ring.

"Hey, did you change your mind? Are you coming back to get me?" Emily asked.

"No," she said. Anna cleared her throat. "I need you to get the van and come get me. Something happened."

"Oh my God. I knew you shouldn't have been driving. Are you okay? Where are you?"

"Two, maybe three miles from the estate. It wasn't me, Emily. I was fine to drive, but something's wrong with the car. The brakes stopped working. I nearly lost control..."

There was a long pause on the other end of the line.

"Anna, are you sure?"

"Of course I am. Why?" she asked.

"Because I checked over the whole car from top to bottom, including the rotors, pads, lines, and fluids two days ago. That thing was in pristine condition. There is no reason you shouldn't have brakes unless..."

"Unless what?"

"Nothing. I don't think we need to get into it on the phone. I'm just happy you are okay. We're going to figure this out. I'll take a look at the Impala and see what's going on. Listen, I'm going to grab Peter, and I'll be there in a minute, okay? Just sit tight."

"What were you going to say, Emily? You can't start to say something like that and then cut yourself off," Anna said.

She sighed. "All right, fine. If you didn't do anything and if I checked it and made sure it was good to go, that only leaves one possible scenario for what's happening. Someone tampered with the car."

Her stomach lurched. The idea that someone was trying to harm them had never crossed her mind. Now they knew about Nancy and Janice, though, and everything was different. If someone was trying to harm them, they needed to get as far away from the estate as possible, but even as Anna thought it, she knew Emily would never agree. Her friend wasn't one to back down from a fight, and before long, Anna worried it was going to get them killed. Whatever was happening, it was clear that Emily and Anna were being caught in the crossfire.

"Let's just get a tow truck here and get it to a mechanic. I'm sure it's nothing like that."

"We don't need a mechanic. Peter and I are on our way now. I'll be able to tell you what's going on as soon as I get there. Just hold tight, okay?"

"It's not like I can go anywhere," she grumbled.

Emily chuckled. "Listen, I'm just happy you are okay. I don't care about that car or about the house when it comes down to it. Keeping you safe is my only priority right now."

"Me? What about you? You're in just as much danger as I am."

Emily hesitated. "Anna, I don't think I am. All of this stuff that keeps happening? It's happening to you. I don't think anyone is after me because my name isn't on the deed. You need to be careful and take this seriously, okay?"

"Yeah," she whispered. "I know."

"I'll see you in a minute. It's going to be okay."

Ending the call with Emily, she looked down at her trembling hands. Anna knew it was the fear causing her to shake, and it was no longer fatigue. Coming to terms with what had just happened was going to take time, but the fear would linger for as long as she allowed it. It didn't seem possible that their lives had taken such a dramatic turn, and yet they were fighting for survival. It was becoming clear that someone or *something* didn't want her to unravel the mystery of the Harrington house.

35

Anna's heart was racing with the idea that something or someone didn't want her to get to the truth. Although from the aspect of someone on the outside looking in, it might have seemed like a trivial thing, she felt that there was something darker working in the shadows around her. In the moment, nothing else mattered. There wasn't anything that was going to stop her from getting to the bottom of the true story behind the estate and the people who had died there. As long as she was alive and kicking, she was going to do everything in her power to get to the truth behind it all. The car was sitting on the side of the road, and she was leaning up against the passenger side, away from any of the traffic that might come down the path she was taking. Suddenly, she heard a vehicle approaching and looked down the road just in time to see Emily arriving with Peter and Justin.

There was a part of her that felt foolish for needing to call for help, but she had no other choice. As her three rescuers climbed out of Peter's truck, she simply nodded and stepped away from the car, spreading both of her arms out in a display of confusion. Emily was the first one to make it to her and wrapped her in a big hug, obviously thankful that nothing worse had happened. Peter and Justin were right behind her, and it was clear they both were thankful she was all right, although Justin was already looking around the car, trying to get an idea of what had happened.

"I'm not sure what is going on with the car," Anna said.

"Can you just give me an idea of what it did?" Justin asked.

"It's more like what it didn't do. I was just driving down the road and suddenly didn't have any brakes. They didn't go all the way out at first, but the pedal gradually became softer the harder I pressed them."

"Sounds like you have a brake fluid leak. It's not all that uncommon on these older vehicles, but I'll climb under and take a look just to be sure."

Anna was thankful that Emily and her new friends had come to save her, but she was confused by the idea that it had been caused by a brake fluid leak. Although she wasn't one to check under the car every time she was about to drive, she was almost certain she had never seen any fluid under the vehicle prior to that moment. As she watched Justin kneel down and look around the underneath of the car, she wondered if it was something simple to fix, since she knew nothing about vehicles. She was looking in the direction of the hill she had almost made it to when she heard the sound of the young man groaning out loud. Her attention was back to Justin, who was climbing back out from underneath the car.

"I was right about the fact that you have brake fluid spraying out from the cylinder, but it looks like it's been cut."

"What does that mean?" Anna asked.

Justin sighed. "The only thing I can tell you for sure is that the leak wasn't caused due to old age. Someone climbed under here and cut your brake line on purpose."

"Are you sure?" Emily asked. "Why would anybody do such a thing?"

"I have no idea. I just know the hose has been cut clean through. There's no way it rotted out or got caught on anything. Someone took the time to climb underneath and cut it with a knife."

Anna was reeling from the news and had no idea who would want to try to kill her. If she had made it just a little farther down the road, there would have been no telling what would have happened to the car or to her. The one thing she was sure of was she had been moments away from possibly ending her life, and the thought sent a shiver down her spine. Justin was curious about the rest of the car and was looking at the rest of the brakes while Peter pulled out his phone and called a friend. He told her he had a buddy who could use his tow truck to haul it back, and although she wasn't certain what they should do next, Emily called the police anyway.

They weren't going to be able to prove it, but Emily insisted they involve the local police so there was a record of what someone had tried to do. Anna wasn't sure if she agreed with what her friend was doing, but it made sense to have a paper trail. The last thing she needed was to have to worry about her car every time she drove, but none of what had happened made any sense in her mind. She was trying to piece together anyone she had angered recently enough for someone to cut her brake lines, but the only person that came to mind was Nancy, who was already doing everything in her power to get the property back. It was a thought she pushed from her mind, knowing there wasn't any chance the woman would try to kill her over the estate.

Once Emily was off the phone with the police department, she made her way over to Anna's side. She had been speechless since finding out the true cause of her almost getting into an accident. She was trying to wrap her mind around it all. As everyone around her continued to make sure the situation was going to be handled properly, Anna found herself looking in the direction of the hill and then back to the car that had nearly gotten her killed. Although it was a sixty-seven Impala and the age alone would make most people view it as a death trap, the handful of times she had driven it came with no issues. It didn't seem plausible that anything other than someone's hate for her had damaged the brake system. Taking a deep breath, she looked around the surrounding area and tried to talk herself out of the anger she was starting to feel about the situation.

It wasn't until a local officer started to pull up that she was able to snap herself out of her own thoughts. She started making her way in the officer's direction, knowing he was going to need a full statement from her. Since there hadn't been any damage to the car or property, she knew the only reason he was there was because Emily had called. Although Nancy was the only person she could think of who would want to harm her in any way, she wasn't sure the woman had it in her. Anna had no idea what she was going to tell the police other than what exactly had happened and what Justin had told her about the brake line. No one was going to be able to do anything about the situation, but she knew Emily was right, and it needed to be on record.

Suddenly, just as the police cruiser came to a stop behind Peter's truck, she noticed another car pulling up as well. As soon as she recognized the car as the one that the mayor drove, she could no longer keep the rage she was feeling inside. It was already bad enough that the only suspect who came to mind was the woman inside the car, but she certainly didn't understand why the woman was following the police to her location and how she had found out about it. Anna started to make her way in the woman's direction, knowing deep in her heart that Nancy had something to do with the brake lines. Although she was trying to give the woman the benefit of the doubt, when she stepped out of the car, along with Janice, she knew something more was going on around her.

As soon as Nancy closed the door and started in her direction, Anna recognized the smug look on the woman's face. It might not have been obvious to anyone else, but she could see not only the look of disdain written all over her face, but it almost looked as though she was happy about the situation. It only seemed to anger her more than she already was, and she was glad when she felt Emily grab her arm to hold her back. At least there was someone else in the group who understood what she was feeling, but the only thing she wanted to do was get her hands on the woman who had almost caused an accident.

36

Nancy and Janice stopped in front of the police cruiser as the officer turned on his flashing lights and started to climb out of his car. Anna was just happy Emily was there to hold her back, although when she glanced over in her friend's direction, the woman was just as angered by the situation as she was. It was clear that both of them were under the understanding that Nancy was the only one who would have it out for either of them, or it could have been either of them behind the wheel at any given time. The thought that not only was her life in danger but also her friend's life sent another surge of rage through her. Anna wasn't sure how it was possible, but as soon as she heard the woman starting to speak, she became angrier than she had ever been before.

"What happened here? Did that old car break down on you?" Nancy asked.

"You should know exactly what happened," Anna snapped. "Don't stand there and pretend that you have no clue what is going on."

The officer cleared his throat. "Do one of you want to tell me what is going on here and what exactly you mean?"

"Nothing. I know I don't have any proof to back up what I think happened."

"It might be a good idea to tell me your thoughts on the matter."

Nancy chuckled. "I wouldn't doubt it if it had something to do with the rumored curse of the place, and since that car was part of the estate, it's probably just as cursed as the rest of it. Maybe you should have gotten out when you had the chance."

Anna started to take a step in the woman's direction, but before she had the chance to move any closer, Emily stepped forward and got right into Nancy's face. Anna was impressed with how fast Emily had moved but even more impressed by the fact that the officer was able to step between them before the entire situation got out of hand. There was some bickering between the two of them, and although Emily was angered by what had happened, it almost seemed as though the two women were amused by the situation. They weren't downright laughing about what had happened, but each of them had a sinister smile on their faces. Just seeing the look that both of them were giving to her was enough to tell her that her thoughts had been correct. One way or another, Nancy was involved with her brakes getting cut.

It took the officer several moments to separate the two women, and Emily never stopped yelling profanity and making other statements in Nancy's direction. To her credit, Nancy took every word in stride, but what bothered her the most was the smile that the woman carried on her face. Anna didn't care how long it took; she was going to have to find the proof she needed to put the woman away. She had taken a step back from the situation, knowing the officer seemed prepared to throw someone in jail at the first sign of trouble. When Emily finally stopped cursing and screaming at the woman, the officer glanced in her direction and shrugged.

"Is there anything you can tell me that will help me find out what is going on here?" the officer asked. "You shouldn't point any fingers unless you have evidence to support your theory."

Anna shook her head. "I don't have any proof other than the fact that I know my brake line was cut."

"Do you happen to know who did it or have any proof that would warrant an investigation into the matter? Even if you saw someone around the car recently who shouldn't have been there, that's enough for me to open an investigation."

"I have worked on enough cars to know what a freshly cut brake line looks like. We obviously don't have any proof as to who is behind it, but I'm certain it was done on purpose."

"There's not much I can do without any evidence to look into a suspect. I can call the tow truck out if you need one. Other than that, it's out of my hands legally."

Peter shook his head. "That won't be necessary. I have a friend of mine coming to pick up the car now."

The officer shrugged. "Suit yourself. If there isn't anything else I can do here, then I'll be on my way."

"You can tell that bitch to stay away from us," Emily snapped.

Nancy scoffed. "Who do you think you are dealing —"

"Maybe you should ask yourself that question. Neither one of you has any idea who you are messing with right now, and I promise you that this isn't over. You could have killed one of us, and the only thing you were worried about is the estate."

Janice sighed. "If you haven't figured it out yet, neither one of you is wanted here. Things are only going to continue to happen until you figure that out."

"Is that a threat?" Anna asked.

"It's just the truth of the matter. There's no way of knowing what type of things are coming, but I know it's not going to stop until you realize that you don't belong in this town."

"Let's break it up," the officer said. "If you need any further assistance, just call the department and they will send someone out."

Anna shook her head. "I think we can handle everything else."

Although she was glad the officer had been there to break things up between the four of them, she was sure he wasn't on their side. He hadn't been obvious about the fact, but he wasn't going to do anything to either Nancy or Janice, even if they had the proof they needed. It didn't take long for the officer to climb back into his cruiser and for the women to get back into their own vehicle. Anna could feel the rage surging inside of herself, but there was nothing she was going to be able to do until she was able to prove who had cut her brake line. For just a moment, she felt like even if she had the proof she needed, nothing was going to happen.

Maybe the woman was right, and maybe it was her own anger blinding her from seeing the truth. Even though there was a possibility that Nancy and Janice were right about the fact that they weren't one of them, the fact that they had been led to the treasure when no one else could find it told her another story. While it was possible that there were many people in the community who didn't want them there, she had a passing thought that people from its history meant for them to be there, whether anyone else liked it or not. Anna was pulled from her thoughts when the cruiser and the car carrying the two other women pulled away. Anna knew if she had a rock in her hand, she most likely would have thrown it through the mayor's windshield in an attempt to show her rage.

Around the time the police cruiser and the women disappeared into the distance, Anna spotted the tow truck. While she was angered by the situation and having almost lost her life, she felt a sense of pride, knowing she had surrounded herself with the type of people who would help her if the need ever came. The tow truck pulled up in front of the Impala and started to hook up to it when she noticed Peter making his way over to where she had been standing. She immediately thanked the man for everything, and he smiled while shaking his head.

"I never have a problem helping a friend in need."

"I'm sure there are other kind people throughout town, but those two seem to have it out for me and Emily."

"I wouldn't put too much stock into anything they ever have to say to you, and any amount of kindness they show you is nothing but a farce."

"What do you mean?"

Peter shrugged. "Honestly, I wouldn't be surprised in the least if they had something to do with your brakes. Both of those women have been crooked for as long as I can remember them being around."

37

Anna's mind was racing from the entire situation to the altercation they'd had with Nancy and Janice. The whole thing had shaken her to her core, knowing she was moments away from ending up on the downside of the hill and possibly wrecking the car. As far as she could remember, she had never been so close to death as in that moment. She was trying to wrap her head around what had happened and why someone would be willing to go to such great lengths to do her harm. It certainly didn't make any sense that someone would be capable of murder over something as simple as a piece of property, but she was starting to understand the amount of trouble they were in when dealing with Nancy and Janice.

It wasn't until she climbed into the vehicle with

Peter and the others that she realized her hands were trembling. The entire situation left her shaken, and as they drove back to the house, she couldn't help but think about what they could do to get rid of the women who were causing so many problems. Anna started to think about the information she already knew, and it was becoming clear that the only way she or Emily were ever going to get out from underneath Janice or Nancy was to prove they had something to do with their husbands' deaths. It wasn't going to be easy, but it was the only possible way they would be able to live without fearing every move they made.

The surrounding silence was driving her mad as Peter drove them back to the estate. Anna knew the only reason everyone else was so quiet was because they were waiting for her to speak, and no one knew exactly what to say. She was sure everyone in the vehicle was on the same page and that everyone knew Nancy had something to do with the brake line being cut. The only problem was they weren't going to be able to get the police to do anything without some sort of evidence, and there was no way to prove she had done anything to the car. When she saw the estate and the house come into view, she was grateful they were almost home.

Just as they started to pull into the driveway and came to a stop near the house, Lori pulled in behind them. She was glad to see the woman, knowing she was not just there for Emily but there to support her as well. Anna had barely climbed out of the car when the woman rushed over to her and wrapped her arms around her. There was a moment of awkwardness, but Anna hugged Lori back before noticing Emily, a few feet away, smiling. Emily had noticed the awkward look on her face, but it was only because there had never been any physical contact between the two of them. When they broke the embrace, Anna couldn't help but smile in return.

As she watched Emily and Lori embrace, she noticed Peter and Justin making their way back to the house, getting right back to work. Anna was glad to have the friends in her life that she had, and she had surrounded herself with the right people. The man and his son had dropped everything to rush to her aid, and Lori was the first person there to greet them and check on her upon their return. Even though there was a lot of work that needed to be done in order to prove the things she was thinking, Anna was starting to wonder if their new friend would be able to help them in any way. Proving that Nancy and Janice had something to do with their husbands' deaths was at the top of her list of things to do, and she wanted to get started as soon as possible.

"I was worried about you when Emily told me that you had almost gotten into an accident. She said something about your brakes being cut?"

Anna nodded. "Justin climbed under the car and said the brake line had been cut clean through."

"Who would do such a thing?"

Emily sighed. "We have no proof, but we have a pretty good idea of who is behind it."

"The way you say that makes me think I know who it is as well. Is there anything I can do for you?"

"We have heard stories about the curse here on the property and other strange things that have happened in the past. I think it will make Anna feel better if we find someone to perform a séance or something like that."

"I mean, I told you I know someone who could do that."

Anna sighed. "If there is any chance that spirits of the past haunt this place, I'm hoping we can get some information from them. Do you know anyone who might be able to help us with that?"

"I already told you it would be a good idea to bring one in and see what kind of answers you can get," Lori said. "If there are spirits here, they will know exactly what to do."

She remembered the conversation they'd had with Lori before and knew it was the only way they were going to be able to get any information about what they were trying to find out. The fact that both men had died on the property and that one of them had been in her dreams was the only way she was going to be able to reach out. With everything that had been going on and the fact that she had almost been in an accident, she had nearly forgotten that the three of them had already talked about holding a séance. She was simply glad that no one was judging her for her slip in memory.

Anna was grateful that Lori would be able to contact someone who could help them, and she was even happier to see that the woman had immediately pulled out her phone and started making calls. It didn't take her long to get in touch with a friend who was more than happy to set up a séance that night. While it was hours away, Anna was glad to see that things were starting to head in the right direction. She was hoping it was only a matter of time before they would have the proof they needed to get rid of the women for good without having to worry about repercussions in the future. As soon as they had set up the appointment for later that evening, they went back to working on the house.

Peter and Justin were already inside with their crew, but she couldn't get over the fact that they needed to find evidence of murder. Although there was plenty of work that needed to be done on the house and the estate in general, there were more than enough people getting their hands dirty. Anna and Emily weren't going to be needed right away. After a short conversation with Lori and Emily, she told them both what she was thinking. Their new friend was taken aback for just a moment, but she understood they had no other choice in the matter. Instead of going back to work on the mansion, they decided to do more research on the estate and try to find anything that would link the women to the deaths in question.

Lori, Anna, and Emily were trying to search for anything they could find online. There wasn't a whole lot of information at first, but they were able to find that both of the men had been extremely wealthy. It explained why Nancy had been able to live outside of her means, which was a question she had asked herself from the beginning. It had been obvious that a mayor wouldn't have the type of income to live the way Nancy did, but Anna had always thought that there was some reason behind it that would make it all make sense. To make matters worse, both of the sisters were each other's alibis on the nights of both of the accidents.

Anna knew it wasn't going to be enough proof to do anything, but she was sure they were covering for each other in one way or another. She tried to put herself in both of their shoes and concluded that if they were ever going to try to get away with murder, Emily would be the perfect alibi for Anna. Anna also knew she would be the perfect alibi for Emily, but they had no way of proving malice on either of their parts. They were going to have to do a lot more digging in order to find the answers to the questions they were asking. Even though a short amount of time had passed, she wasn't ready to give up on the fact that they might be able to find something on the internet. Although the information they had found between the two of them was enough for each of them to come to the same conclusion, it wasn't going to be enough to bring them up on murder charges.

38

Hours passed, and they had been digging up any information they could find on the internet to prove what they all thought. Anna was grateful that no matter how crazy she was starting to feel about the thoughts she was having, she wasn't the only one who felt that way. The more the three of them discussed the different possibilities, the more she realized that Emily and Lori agreed with her. In one way or another, the two women had been responsible for the deaths of their husbands, but they had found it difficult to find any type of proof they could take to the police. Not only did they know Nancy and Janice had something to do with their deaths, one—if not both—of them was responsible for the cut brake line that had caused her to almost crash earlier that day.

Anna was struggling to understand the reason

behind any of it, but she knew more than anything it was simply due to greed. The two women wanted nothing to do with the property until the fortune had been found, and they were either jealous of the fortune or simply thought it belonged to them. Either way, Anna knew there was only one possible way to get rid of them for good, and that was to find the proof they needed. In order to do that, though, they were going to need a medium in order to get their answers from the beyond. It might not be the proof they needed in order to make a case, but at the very least, they knew beyond a shadow of a doubt they were moving in the right direction.

It was almost eight at night when Lori left to pick up the medium. Anna started to get excited as she and Emily set up the table for the séance in the living room. Although she had written about them in the past, Anna had never been a part of one before. The only thing she knew for sure was that the medium would be able to speak to any of the spirits living in the house, even if she had no idea what they were dealing with. As the two of them continued to prepare for the medium to arrive, Anna started to think about how well Emily and Lori were getting along. It was nice that Emily had been able to find someone she could connect with on a romantic level, and Anna wanted to make sure that her friend knew how happy she was about the situation.

"I like Lori," Anna said. "I think the two of you are

perfect for one another, and I'm glad you found her here."

Emily blushed. "I like her a lot. It's a strange thing for me to say, but we have the type of connection I have never felt before. I'm not even sure I could explain it to you if I tried."

"There's no reason to explain it. As long as the two of you feel like it's right and make each other happy, that's all that matters."

"I can honestly say I am happier with her than I have ever been in the past with anyone else. In an odd way, she completes me. I just feel like everything is perfect when we are together."

Anna smiled. "I can sense it every time the two of you are in the same room. I think you are meant to be with each other."

"If you keep that up, you're going to make me all weepy. How are you feeling about the séance? Are you nervous?"

"I am a bit. I know I have written about them in my books before, and I honestly believe they help in certain cases. I just don't know what to expect from this, if anything."

Emily nodded. "That actually makes perfect sense. I think it would be weird if you weren't nervous about it at all, but you have to know there are some spirits here. There's no other way to explain how you dreamed about the location of the hidden fortune."

"I guess so. I think that is more than just the

dreams I've been having, and I believe I have been seeing ghosts this entire time."

"How does that make you feel? I mean, on the one hand, your dream led you to the fortune we found, but on the other hand, I know you have been having terrible nightmares off and on since our arrival here."

Anna thought about it for a few moments and knew Emily was speaking the truth. Everything that had happened since their arrival at the estate had been strange, and there wasn't any other way to explain it. The nightmares she had been having that had kept her awake at night were only the beginning of the things she had been feeling. She knew every sensation of being watched was simply because of the spirits around her, but it almost seemed like something more than that. Although she hadn't been certain of what had led her to the fortune in the beginning, it was the spirits calling to her. It had taken some time to accept it, but she didn't understand why. She wanted to know what had made her special, but she was almost certain she was never going to get that answer.

As the two of them set up the rest of the items they would need for the séance, she couldn't help but feel like they had been brought to the estate for something bigger than themselves. Anna honestly believed they hadn't purchased the winning raffle ticket for no reason, and there wasn't enough luck between them to have won the grand prize. There was something more going on, and for whatever reason, she felt as though the spirits were pulling all the strings. It wasn't something a logical person would conclude, but there wasn't any other answer that made sense. Anna just wanted to find the answers she was looking for, and bringing a medium in was a long shot. Taking a deep breath, she exhaled slowly before answering.

"There's no denying that my dream took us to the location of the hidden fortune and gold bars, but it's strange and very unsettling to know I'm seeing ghosts."

Emily nodded. "I imagine it would be, but do you have any idea what any of it means?"

Anna chuckled softly. "The only thing I know for sure is it means we have a ton of money now, but other than that, I don't know anything. I definitely think we were brought here for a reason."

"You don't think it was a coincidence?"

"Have you ever felt lucky enough to win the lottery?"

Emily smiled and shrugged. "I don't think either one of us has ever had that kind of luck, but I have no idea what would make a spirit think we could help at all."

"That's why I'm hoping that bringing in a medium will give us the answers we are looking for. The only thing I can think of is that the spirits want the truth to come out, and they have been reaching out in the only way they know how."

"That's kind of creepy, if you think about it."

"I didn't say my answer was going to make sense. I just have no other way of explaining all the things that have been happening or why we are here. There is no chance that this is all just a coincidence, and I have to believe that the spirits are trying to tell us something."

Emily smiled. "Maybe this séance will give us the answers we are looking for, but what are we going to do with the information if it is something far more heinous than we could ever dream about?"

"As long as I know we are on the right path, I'll do whatever I have to do in order to put Nancy and Janice away for the rest of their lives."

Her friend just nodded, and they went back to work getting the rest of the table set up for the séance. Anna knew it was strange they were going to be trying to speak to the dead, but she had done enough research in the past for her novels to know that it was a possibility. She had never been a firm believer in ghosts, but her thoughts on the matter had changed since their arrival at the estate. There was no other way to explain things that had happened since they had come to the area, and she just hoped that the medium that Lori was bringing was good enough to break the barrier between the real world and the afterlife. More than anything, she wanted to get to the truth behind all the strange occurrences that had happened at the mansion throughout history.

39

Shortly after they had finished setting up the table, Lori came back with the medium. Anna had been so lost in thought since the conversation with her friend that she almost didn't hear the woman walk in, but when she looked up, she was shocked to see the medium was a man and not a woman at all. In every novel she had written about the supernatural and dealing with the spirit world, she had made the character a woman. The man could easily speak to the dead as well. She had never met a man who did the job. Without meaning to be, she became skeptical about his ability, and although he looked to be in his late fifties, it wasn't immediately clear how much experience he had. Lori smiled as she approached and introduced the man.

"This is Samuel the Seeker," she said.

"It's nice to meet you, but I have to admit I was kind of expecting a woman," Anna said.

Samuel smiled. "I'm sure you wouldn't be surprised to hear that happens more frequently than I would like. I can assure you I am more than capable of making the connection you are looking for."

"I didn't mean it that way. I just know most of the people that do this sort of thing are women, and I even write them that way in my books."

"It's true. Most of the people I have met during my life that do this sort of thing are women, but I think that just gives me the extra power I need to talk to the afterlife."

Emily chuckled. "Do you believe the doubt people have in you is something that fuels your ability?"

Samuel nodded. "There's no way other way to explain it. I have been doing this for many years, and I have always made contact with the spirits people are asking me to reach out to. Never once has my ability failed me, and I can assure you that this is going to be no different."

"What makes you so sure?"

The man simply smiled and shook his head before he moved to the head of the table and sat down. Anna was aware that the entire situation was a little creepy, but they had no other choice but to move forward with the man. There wasn't anyone else they could reach out to, and she was tired of waiting for answers. As she looked around the room, she felt a strange feeling wash over her. Even though there were three others around her, she felt like there was more. It became clear that whatever spirits were haunting the estate were standing there with them, and although they were moments away from performing a séance, it felt strange to say anything out loud.

No matter how hard she tried to change the way she felt, Anna was skeptical. She looked over at Emily, and it was clear that she felt the same way. Lori simply chuckled, grabbing their attention before they all sat at the table. Emily sat on Anna's right side, and Lori sat on her left, with Samuel sitting directly across from her. It made no difference whether a woman led the séance, but it was simply something she was unaccustomed to. The only experience she had with a medium was from her own research and what she had written in her novels, but she had no idea what to expect. As the four of them got settled in, Lori smiled in her direction.

"You should know Samuel only does séances for people who have already spoken to him before," Lori said.

"What do you mean?"

Samuel smiled. "Neil Thomas reached out to me several weeks ago. I believe he has been trying to reach out for quite some time."

"I don't understand how that is possible," Emily said.

"When spirits have something to say, they seek out

those who can hear them. Neil reached out to me several weeks ago, and it's the reason I didn't hesitate to come over."

"What did he say?"

"I guess we are just going to have to find out together, aren't we?"

There was silence at the table for several seconds, and she tried to wrap her mind around what she had just been told. Anna knew at that moment that everything she had been feeling was right. The estate had many hidden secrets that the spirits wanted to come out, and she was glad they had finally decided to go through with the séance. She tried to push every thought from her mind and focus on what they were about to do. If everything went according to plan, they were moments away from hearing all the secrets the estate was holding. She was excited by what they could learn.

In the world of spirits she wrote about in her novels, ghosts always had a way of getting the truth out to the rest of the world. Anna was also aware that spirits would reach out to those who could talk to them, hoping to find a release from the world they were trapped in. If they were able to get to the truth, the spirits would be free to move on to the afterlife the way things were intended. She took a deep breath before exhaling slowly and focused on the man sitting at the other end of the table. Although she had never met a medium who was a man, as she looked into Samuel's eyes, her faith in his ability began to grow.

There were several moments of awkward silence within the group, aside from the sounds and words that Samuel was speaking. Anna was trying to keep herself focused on what they were doing, but she felt like her skeptical thoughts were holding her back. Once she was finally able to push all of those thoughts from her mind, she felt a strange sensation run through her body and a chill go down her spine. The lights in the room began to flicker, and although she was trying not to lose focus, she opened her eyes long enough for the entire room to go dark, aside from the single candle they had sitting in the middle of the table.

It was one thing to write a story about what they were doing, but it was entirely different actually being in the same room where a séance was taking place. Anna found it impossible to describe what she was feeling, but there was obviously something else in the room with them. She couldn't stop staring at the candle in the middle of the table, knowing it was their only source of light. Even though they were sitting in the dining room with all the windows closed, she could feel the air moving all around her. She was sure she wouldn't have been able to describe the sensation washing over her if anyone asked, but she was so intent on getting to the truth that she couldn't say a word.

Samuel continued with whatever prayer or words he was saying out loud until the flickering of the candle was the only thing that could be heard. Everything in the room came to a complete stop, and no sound was made. As she continued to focus on the candle, she realized the only thing she could hear was the popping of the candle wick. Suddenly, the lights came back on and were much brighter than they were supposed to be. She could hear the humming of the bulbs all around her, and the light was so bright that she had to squint to see through the room.

Anna glanced around at the others, but none of them were looking at her, except for Samuel, who was staring right at her. No one said a thing, but when the flame coming from the top of the candle grew exponentially, everyone immediately looked in its direction. Without warning, the entire room was dark again, and the candle had been blown out. Although there was no normal explanation for what she had just witnessed, Anna was starting to think Samuel was a fake and that the whole thing wasn't going to get them anywhere. All of a sudden, the darkness in the room was filled with the candle once again, as the flame started all on its own.

40

For just a moment, she thought she felt the presence of someone behind her, but her focus was entirely on the flame flickering in front of her face. The flame that sat on top of the candle continued to grow. Anna could see the flame separating from the candle itself as the fire started to float several inches above the wick. It was one of the craziest things she had ever seen, and her heart was pumping harder than it ever had before. Any doubt she had in Samuel's ability was gone, but she was wondering what was going to happen next. The fire was floating in midair, several feet above where the candle sat. In reality, she knew what she was witnessing was impossible, but she also understood that whatever was causing the flame to float was in the room with them.

Just as quickly as the fire had separated from the

candle, it slammed back onto the table, causing her to lean backward in her chair. Anna almost started to laugh at herself before she realized that the entire room was pitch black, and she was all alone. The revelation sent fear through her body, and there were a few more seconds of silence before she heard the sound of something moving behind her. If she didn't know any better, she would have thought someone was standing directly behind her chair. It wasn't until she felt air moving around her right ear and heard the sound of a man whispering her name that she spun around in her chair, not ready for what was standing in front of her when she did.

At first, Anna had no idea what she was seeing. It felt as though the entire room around her was gone, but she could tell she was in the dining room. The pitch black that swallowed the immediate air around her made it difficult to see anything. When everything finally started to come together, she saw the man who had been in her dreams standing in front of her. It felt like the room was going to swallow her whole, and although she was terrified, she swallowed hard and looked the man directly in his eyes. He was no longer a man but a spirit and the type of things they were known for. Stories she had read in the past told her they could be dangerous, and she had no idea what kind of spirit she was dealing with. Some of them were no more than kindhearted souls stuck between worlds, while others were hateful and vengeful, creating all kinds of havoc.

Most people would have tried to get away, and she wasn't sure if it was because of the fear she was feeling in her heart or the fact that she wanted to help was causing her to stay, but she wasn't going anywhere. Anna wanted to get to the bottom of what had happened, not only to him but to the others as well. There was a whistling sound that surrounded them both, and it felt like there wasn't another person in the room. Even as she turned her head slightly to look toward the others, they were nowhere to be found. She could feel her heart racing and the pounding sound from it pumping rang in her ears, but she forced herself to look back at the man who had appeared behind her. There was sadness in his eyes, but there was something else there as well.

Anna had a ton of questions lined up when they had first decided to perform the séance, but at that moment, she couldn't think of a single word to say to the man. The only thing she wanted was the truth. She wanted to know what had happened to everyone and find a way to set them free. Spirits were nothing more than lost souls who were trapped on earth because of unfinished business, and even though it was the first time she had ever dealt with a ghost, Anna wanted nothing more than to help release him from his pain. She wasn't even sure what she was going to say until the words started to come from her mouth.

"We just want to help you," Anna said. "We want to help release you and free you from being trapped here."

"There are others."

"All we want to do is help set all of you free."

"It's far too late for any of us to be saved. If you know what's good for you, you should leave as well. You should go before it's too late for you and Emily."

"I don't understand," Anna said. "Samuel said you reached out to him, and I know you want the truth out for everyone to see."

The man nodded. *"The truth will set everyone free, and it is the only justice there is."*

"Let me help you, then. Tell me the truth you are looking to tell. Allow me to be the one who sets all of you free. It's never too late for the truth. The only thing we are here to do is make things right."

The sadness in the man's eyes gave Anna a direct link to see into the man's soul. While he was trying to scare them away from whatever he thought might happen, he was just as scared as she was. Whatever they had done to him and whatever reason was keeping him from moving on to the other side, she had to get to the bottom of it. They shared a look. They understood each other for just a moment before he started to fade away. Anna didn't know what to say in order for the spirit to believe her, but she wasn't ready to give up on any of the lost souls.

Somehow, she felt like time was running out. It wasn't just the time she was going to have with the man in front of her; it was something stronger than that. Anna suddenly felt the same way she had when she had almost gotten into an accident earlier that day. There was something changing around her, but she had no way to explain it. She pushed every thought from her mind and focused on the spirit in front of her, trying to find a way to make him understand they were there to help. The only way the spirits were ever going to be set free was by making whatever had gone wrong right. It was going to be impossible to do if he wouldn't tell her what she needed to know.

"There's nothing you can do for us."

"Please, just tell me the truth, and I will find a way to set you free from here," she pleaded.

"The truth is going to set us all free, and justice is the only way to find that truth."

Without warning, the spirit disappeared, leaving her lost as the murderous events played in her mind's eye. There, she saw everything Janice and Nancy had done. Somewhere far off in the distance and in the darkness, she heard Emily shouting her name, distracting her from the visions in her head. Nothing felt right at that moment, and she realized she was staring up while lying on her back. It wasn't until the world around her started to come back into focus that she understood she had been knocked backward in her chair and was looking at the ceiling above her. The darkness that had so filled the room was gone, and in its place was the light that had disappeared before.

Emily kneeled beside her, and then she looked around the room. Lori and Samuel were standing above her as well. It wasn't like she had gone anywhere, but she could see the concerned looks on all of their faces. It came as a shock to her that everyone was so worried about her, and she wondered what they had seen to cause such concern. Emily helped her to her feet as she was trying to gain her bearings. She had no idea what had just happened, but she remembered everything the man had said to her. The spirit was more worried about Anna and Emily getting away than he was about freeing himself. It was a question in her mind that wouldn't go away, but she wasn't going to give up so easily.

41

"How did I end up on the floor?" Anna asked.

"The entire room went dark for several seconds, aside from the candle sitting in the middle of the table. As soon as the lights came back on, you were sitting in the chair, but the chair was lying on his back on the floor," Emily said.

"That doesn't make any sense."

"What do you mean? That's exactly what happened from our point of view."

"Are you telling me I was only in the dark for a couple of seconds?"

Emily nodded. "I'd say it was only three seconds at most. The rest of the time, you were in a complete trance. What happened to you?"

"I spoke to Neil."

"What did he say?"

"I told him we were here to help free him from being trapped, but he simply told me that the truth was the only justice that would set anyone free. He warned me we needed to leave as soon as possible before it was too late for us."

"Anytime you receive a warning from a spirit, you should heed that warning," Samuel said.

Anna nodded, knowing it would have been the logical thing to do. She was already thinking about the next thing they needed to do in order to save themselves. After promising her friend several times she was just fine, Emily walked Lori and Samuel to the door. She thanked them before they left the room, but she was busy planning the next step. Anna didn't want to go into too much with the others there, but that was exactly what she needed to do in order to make Nancy and Janice pay for the things they had done.

Emily was gone for several minutes, but Anna knew she was spending a few extra minutes with Lori. It didn't bother her, since it gave her a little time to plot what she was going to do next. She knew exactly how dangerous the two women could be, and she didn't have to know the truth to understand what they were capable of. The only way she was going to be able to get either woman to admit to what they had done was to make them believe it was safe to do so. It was a plan that had several holes in it, but she was confident she would be able to get them to speak the truth and end the reign of terror they had commanded for so long. By the time Emily came back from seeing the others out, she had developed a good portion of the plan in her mind.

"It's obvious you've been thinking about something," Emily said. "Would you care to share?"

Anna nodded. "The only way we are going to get to the bottom of this and get the truth is to make them believe it is safe to confess."

"How do you plan on doing that?"

"I have a pretty good idea, but I need to find a way to get both of them here in order to make it work."

Emily smiled. "I have the perfect way to get them here. I think it's time we end things once and for all. What exactly did you see when you were in that trance?"

"I saw Neil. Everything else around me was like I wasn't even in the same room anymore, but he was standing as close as you and I are now. It seemed like the only thing he was worried about was making sure the two of us were safe."

"What is he so scared of?"

"I could sense fear in him, but I don't think it was fear for himself. I have to believe he knows what Nancy and Janice are capable of."

Emily nodded. "I think we are all aware of that. Are you sure that bringing them here is the best idea? I mean, we already know they have killed before and tried to kill one of us."

"It's the only way we can end this."

Her friend was a little concerned about having both of the sisters at the estate, but after talking for just a little while longer, Anna was able to make her understand it was the only way. She couldn't deny she was concerned about the situation herself, but she had faith she would be able to get both of them talking just as long as they were at the mansion. She had no idea what was giving her that belief, but they were getting closer to finally being able to get rid of Janice and Nancy. It was the only way they were going to be able to live without any fear.

Anna spent several minutes reassuring Emily that once the women were at the estate, everything else was going to be just fine. Something in the back of her mind told her the spirits weren't going to let anything happen to them, and although she was fearful, she knew things were going to end the way they needed to end. The two of them immediately sat at the table and started hashing out the details of the plan. She wasn't exactly sure what they were going to do in order to get the women to talk, but she felt like as long as the two women thought they had the upper hand, they would admit everything to them, thinking they were going to get away with it all. As she told Emily about the scheme she had been cooking up, the look on the woman's face showed Emily wasn't as sure as Anna was.

"If they think they can just kill us both after

confessing, they are going to be ready to talk nonstop," Anna said.

"I just can't stop thinking about how dangerous this is."

"You and I both know they have killed before, but I need you to trust me."

"I do trust you, but I'm not so certain about the rest of your idea."

"All we need to do is get them here. Everything else will take care of itself."

Emily sighed. "I feel like there's something you're not telling me about this trance you were in."

"I told you everything I saw and all of what I heard. I honestly believe the spirits aren't going to let anything happen to either one of us. The only thing they want is the truth to come out and to get justice for what happened to them."

"Do you believe they are going to protect us?"

"Think about it. What other reason would they have to bring us here? They showed us where the treasure was hidden while they kept it from the others for all those years."

"I hadn't thought of it that way. You know you always hear about evil spirits and hauntings but not about them helping out. I guess that if you trust them, I have no choice but to trust them, too. I just hope they know we're the good guys…they do, right?" Emily asked.

Anna smiled and nodded. "I think they do. We don't need to be afraid."

She was glad she had finally found the words were just enough to calm her friend. They immediately went back to work, planning out what they needed to do. Between the two of them, they decided the following evening would be the best time to put their plan into action. It would give them just enough time to prepare everything they needed, and they would be ready for anything the women tried. She almost felt like the spirits were talking through her at times, and she felt like they were finally going to be able to set the ghosts free and move on with their own lives.

42

"I can't believe they are both coming. How did you manage to talk them into it?" Emily asked.

She shrugged. "I was honest with them. I told them I was tired of being somewhere I wasn't wanted, I was constantly terrified of whatever was in this place. Basically, I told them I wanted it all to end."

"Huh, I never thought of that..."

"Of course, I lied a little, too. I have no intention of talking about selling it back to them or donating it to the town like they want. Honestly, it was a struggle for me to lie. You know how much I dislike that," Anna said.

"Be that as it may, it's a good thing you did. I can't imagine they would come if you had told them the entire truth. So, you think they will show up?" Emily asked.

Anna didn't need to think about it as she nodded. The temptation for the two women to get the property back was more than they would be able to pass up. She hated that they were putting themselves in danger, but she knew that was the only way. The longer they stayed at the estate, the more likely it was that neither of them was going to make it out alive. Anna wanted to believe that Emily would be safe from the women's actions but knew they were killers and would stop at nothing to get what they wanted. Anna refused to let Emily be in danger, and she refused to give up the property she rightfully owned simply because the pair thought they could bully her into doing so. She had come to love the land and the community, despite Nancy and Janice's best efforts to ostracize her.

"Well, we have spent a small fortune on cameras and audio recorders for this event, so I hope it pays off," Emily said.

"Even if we can't get them to admit what they have done—and something tells me we'll have help in doing that—we needed the cameras to keep this place safe anyway. Granted, we could probably go without the audio, but it's not the end of the world," Anna said.

They had a little time before the pair were expected to arrive, but all the work was otherwise done. It was now a waiting game. One way or another, they were going to get answers. As Emily sat across from her. Anna could feel her friend's gaze upon her and looked up. Whatever her friend was after, despite having told Emily a half dozen times that she didn't want to discuss it, she could tell Emily wasn't going to let it go. Anna knew her friend deserved answers as much as she did. It wasn't fair that she had gotten them, thanks to the séance, while Emily had been left in the dark.

"You aren't going to let this go, are you?"

"Nope. I want to know what happened to you during that trance. It sure as hell scared the daylights out of me. I just want to know these spirits aren't leading us on a suicide mission."

Anna sighed. She had run out of excuses. Plus, depending on how the next hour went, things were about to transpire that would make no sense to Emily unless she had the whole story. The last thing she wanted was for her friend to be frightened, and after what Anna had seen in her dreams and during the trance, she knew just how terrifying the world of the dead could be. It wasn't for the faint of heart. They had to be on the same page if they were going to make it.

"I wish there was a way to explain what happened, but it was like a dream. At first, I thought I was dead, but then I realized I could hear all of you sitting around the table and talking. It was like my body was with you but my mind was somewhere else. Like my spirit was in another place. If we are being honest, it was the single most bizarre sensation I have ever felt. I don't think there are words to describe it, but it was strange."

"What did you see?" Emily asked.

"I saw it all, everything. I saw her push her husband down the steps, and I saw the other one pulling the trigger in the forest behind the estate. It was awful. I could feel the men's pain as they died. The women had no remorse for what they did. There was nothing but cold, calculating aim on both of their parts. I don't ever want to feel how those poor bastards felt again."

"That sounds awful. I am so sorry you experienced that. I wish it had been me seeing it. You wouldn't have to keep reliving it," Emily said.

Anna shook her head. "No, it had to be me. I am the one Claymont Harrington picked to find the money, and I am the one who is getting the dreams. I honestly think it had to be the person whose name was on the deed before they could reach out."

"That would make sense. No one is going to try to reach out to Nancy or Janice from the great beyond. One of them had to be on the deed before," Emily said.

"There was something else as well. Something after I watched the men die. I don't know how to explain it, but it was like they were talking to me inside my head. I heard their voices, and I heard them asking me to bring the women here to offer them the retribution and vengeance they have been denied for so long. I am a little worried about that."

"Why? If the spirits want to drag them out of here kicking and screaming, I think we should let them. They deserve whatever they have coming to them," Emily said.

Anna shook her head but didn't say anything in reply. She couldn't fathom letting any harm come to the sisters even after everything they had done, at least not if it was in her control. She had a moral compass that wouldn't be swayed otherwise. Anna understood where Emily was coming from. The women had caused chaos in their lives ever since they had arrived at the estate. It didn't help to know they were responsible for the deaths of two men. They had somehow managed to corrupt an entire community. She refused to believe that people couldn't change their lives and turn things around. There was no more time to talk about their strategy as a knock on the door made them both jump. Together, they moved to the entrance, opening the door for the women and casually inviting them in well, hoping their cover wasn't blown.

"To be honest, I wasn't surprised in the least to get your call, Anna. I do think it's a little inappropriate for your friend to be here. She has no purpose in these proceedings," Nancy said.

"She is just here as a witness to everything. I am hoping we can be civil about this, but my hopes aren't very high. I am sure you can understand why."

"Excuse me? We have been nothing but courteous to you since you both first arrived. It's you who has been the rude one. You have been throwing around wild accusations that do nothing for our reputations!" Janice barked.

"Easy now, ladies," Nancy said. "We are all here to work this out as friendly neighbors. After all, Janice, Anna does want to be rid of the property. Let's encourage her in that direction."

"You are right, Mayor. Why don't we take a seat and get this show on the road? After all, one more person never hurt anything," Janice said.

Watching the pair exchange a haunting and knowing look toward each other, Anna knew at that moment they had no intention of letting Emily or Anna leave the property without what they came for. A chill ran down her spine as she considered the lives they had already taken. One way or another, things were going to change forever at the Harrington house that evening. All she could do was pray the tide would turn in their favor.

They had to continue the façade. Plastering a smile on her face, she led the pair to the sitting room off the main foyer. As the foursome took their seats, Anna could almost feel the tension in the air growing. As a breeze moved across the room, she knew they were not alone. The murderous sisters were about to come face to face with those they had slain.

43

"Well then, let's get on with it," Janice said. "We don't have all night, you know. Some of us have real jobs that require skill, not just posting silly videos on the internet. Honestly, it's no wonder you two didn't make it as business owners. I hope you don't expect us to pay for all the renovations that you have done to this place. There is a good chance after this disaster, it will be demolished."

Emily chuckled and shook her head. "Of course that is what you would want to see happen to this place. Unfortunately, I don't think things are going to go exactly how you had planned them."

Janice shook her head. "I don't understand why she is here. Especially if she is going to be rude. We were told that this was a discussion about offloading the estate. I have half a mind to leave right now…"

As Janice started to stand, there was a gust of wind. Suddenly, the door leading from the sitting room to the main foyer slammed shut. Janice and Nancy both jumped, right along with Emily. Anna, though, had been anticipating some sort of retaliation from the spirits. They were there to be heard, and nothing was going to stand in their way. Emily shook her head and smiled, though Anna knew her friend was scared deep down. They had always talked about spirits, but seeing them in action for the first time was a wild ride. She remembered the feeling well.

"What in the hell is going on here? Is this some sort of ruse?" Nancy snapped.

Anna shook her head. "Nope, no ruse. I do think you should sit back down, though, Janice. There are some people here who would like to talk with the two of you."

"I think we've heard enough. You are obviously messed up in the head. We are leaving, and don't think we'll come running the next time you decide this place is too much for you, young lady," Nancy said.

"Too much for me? Oh, I think you've misread the situation. See, this place isn't too much for us, but it does have some secrets, ones that just won't stay buried no matter how much you try to pile dirt on top of them," Anna said. "Tell me, what secrets of yours do you think it's hiding?"

"What are you talking about?" Nancy said.

Anna could tell that the strange happenings at the estate were starting to mess with her head. Janice, though, seemed unbothered by the conversation. Anna knew Nancy was going to be the one to break first. Training her attention on the small-town mayor, Anna smiled. She could feel the eyes of the dead upon them, waiting and watching to play their part. There would be no happy ending for the woman. It was well past time for them to pay for their sins.

"We know, Nancy. We know about your husband, and we know about Janice's. You see, you were right about one thing that first day we met: this place was special. This place has something that most could only dream of."

Janice snorted. "Yeah, a lunatic owner and her angry sidekick."

"The dead," Anna said. "They'd like to talk with you, Nancy. They want to know why you did it. Why did you kill him? Was it the money? Was it the shame of being married to a man with no money, no *Harrington* blood?"

The woman paled slightly. "How did you know about that?"

"He told me—well, I should say he showed me. They both did, actually. I know all about their murders, about your plans to sell this place, then drive out the new owners, to demolish it, and any proof that might be lying around of what you did all those years ago—"

"Nancy, don't say anything to these loons. They are nothing, and they've got nothing. They're trying to goad us," Janice growled.

Anna shook her head. "No, Janice, I'm not trying to goad you or anything else. Just see to it that justice is served, and right now, things aren't looking too good for you."

The woman shook her head and started to stand. Suddenly, she slammed back down in her seat, her eyes growing wide with fear as she fought against the invisible force working to hold her down. It was both terrifying and amazing to behold, knowing the dead had reached out beyond their plane to get answers. A flicker of fear moved across Janice's face as she slowly sat back down next to her sister.

"Nancy, come on, we need to go. Get up," she snarled.

"I-I can't. Something is holding me down. It feels like hands…like Neil's hands on me again—"

"Fine, if you want to stay here, then you can, but I'm leaving," she said.

The woman tried to get up, tried to move, but she, too, was pinned down. Anna and Emily sat quietly across from them, watching it all unfold as though they were simple bystanders. Once more, Janice tried to stand, but she was unable to do so, and Anna knew it was her husband who was keeping her planted in her seat. The fear was growing inside of them, the knowledge that they weren't going to get out of there without the truth being set free.

"All we want is answers," Anna said. "We are not here to pass judgment or to make a scene."

"How are you doing this? What kind of trick are you trying to pull? We were both cleared of the deaths. You can look at the—"

Nancy stopped mid-sentence, gasping instead as Ryan's spirit started to materialize behind her. Anna's hand shot out beneath the table, taking Emily's as they watched. The ghost, transparent but visible, was hunched down over Nancy, whispering into her ear. The woman had started to tremble, a fear now gripping her. Anna could only surmise it was stronger than any she'd ever felt before. She understood the woman's complete terror. The dead were supposed to stay dead, after all.

"Oh my God…" Nancy whispered.

"The truth, Nancy, that's all they want. There is time for you to fix all of this, but Ryan needs to know the truth. He cannot rest until it's out in the open. We don't want you to pay for what you've done, only come clean," Anna said.

"I…this can't be happening. No one was ever supposed to know. I'm so sorry, Ryan. It was right after I'd been elected, and…"

"Just tell them, Nancy," Janice growled. "Tell them what they want so we can get out of here."

"I was pregnant… I'd only found out the week

before, but somehow Ryan found out about it. I'd planned on keeping it a secret and going to Houston to have it taken care of. When he found out, we fought—"

The spirit leaned down again, once more whispering into the woman's ear. She shuddered, a tear slipping down her cheek as she squeezed her eyes shut and tried to ignore the spirit.

"All right! Fine. Ryan wanted to keep it. He'd always wanted to be a father, but I never wanted kids. We just came up here to talk. He'd brought his hunting rifle because a few of the locals had seen sick coyotes up this way. He was trying to do the right thing, but we argued. He threatened to tell my constituents I was going to get an abortion... It was my right, you know."

"And what about Ryan's body?" Anna snapped. "What about his choice to keep living? You didn't care about what happened to him, only yourself...isn't that right?"

"I'm sorry, okay? I'm so sorry it happened. We were arguing, and he saw a coyote. He went to shoot it but missed. When he turned back, I just grabbed the gun and pleaded with him not to tell the locals, not to ruin my political chances, but he wouldn't listen to me. He wanted a divorce if I got rid of the fetus. Ryan tried to take the gun from me, and I don't know... My fingers must have slipped."

Behind her, the ghastly figure of her husband once

more leaned down, but that time, he didn't speak, instead running a putrid finger down her cheek. Though Nancy couldn't see what the spirit was doing, the effects were clear as she started to gag, her eyes once more threatening tears.

"Okay!" she screamed. "It wasn't an accident! I knew where the trigger was, and I shot him, okay? I shot him to protect myself. Then I dragged his body to the creek, buried the gun by the maple groves, and left. I'm so sorry… Ryan, if you can hear me, I'm sorry about what I did. I shouldn't have let my emotions get the best of me, and I didn't know you'd be trapped here all this time. If I could go back in time and take it all away, I would. I'd do everything differently," Nancy stammered.

For the first time, Anna believed what the woman was saying. She could see the fear and regret lingering in Nancy's gaze, but she wasn't sure if it was remorse or if she was simply upset about being caught. They didn't have to wait long to get their answers. Ryan's spirit let go of her. He looked at Anna and smiled for the first time as he disappeared into thin air. She knew he'd finally gotten the peace he so rightly deserved.

44

Next to Nancy, Janice snorted and shook her head. "Wow, so that's all it takes to get rid of these things? A little therapy session? Fine then, if that's what you want, Neil, I'll give it to you."

Anna shook her head. "I don't think that's what he wants—"

"Oh, shut up. This is all your fault, to begin with," Janice snapped. "I don't know how you're doing this, but I refuse to believe any of this is real. What, do you have weights hidden somewhere? Glue on the seats? You know none of this, not even her little confession, is going to hold up in a court of law."

Anna knew there was no point in trying to reason with the woman, to try to get her to believe it wasn't all a ruse. She could believe whatever she wanted, and it wouldn't change a thing. The spirits at the estate weren't working for Anna. They weren't tied there in the hopes of seeing modern justice served; they wanted the truth, and nothing was going to stand in their way.

"I don't care if you ever see the inside of a jail cell. The only reason Emily and I are here is because the spirits needed us to bring you here. We've got no say in your fates. That's up to them now," Anna said.

Janice snorted and stood once more, chuckling and shaking her head at the ease of it when her sister seemed to be pinned to her seat. Glaring at the pair, she casually started to stroll for the door when suddenly, Neil's ghost materialized in front of her. Janice stopped, glaring back at Anna in disbelief before taking another step forward into the man. Suddenly, she ricocheted back, flying several feet through the air and then landing hard on the floor near the back corner of the room. The swift movement made all of them jump, and Emily squeezed her hand for reassurance. Though Anna's heart was racing, she was certain the spirits meant the friends no harm.

"For God's sake, Janice, just tell him what he wants to know!" Nancy screamed.

For the first time, Anna saw true fear in Janice's gaze, but it was short-lived. As she climbed off the floor, using the wall as support, her stare turned to one of indignation. The glares she shot the ghost of her husband would have killed him all over again had he not already been dead. For the first time, Anna felt a twinge of anxiety, but it wasn't because of the undead. Instead, it was living, which appeared to be the threat.

"Wow, Neil, it is you. Well, you don't look like a day over twenty-five, at least," she said. Janice chuckled. "See, I did you a favor. You're immortalized forever in your youth. Look at how old I've gotten! Hell, you should be thanking me."

The spirit took a step closer to her, and the woman's cocky grin faltered. She took a step back, a limp now evident from where the entity had sent her soaring across the room. Nancy chuckled and reached out toward the ghost, her hand moving through it as the color drained from her face. Yet, the woman refused to look afraid. She refused to show any remorse as her sister had done. Anna knew what was coming next and braced herself.

"Okay, all right, maybe what I did was wrong, but come on, you have to admit that things weren't good with us, Neil. I tried to get you to see reason; I did. This place could have been a gold mine for us! I wanted you to come to see its potential, but all you did was point out the flaws and the work it would take. You never supported me, Neil…"

The spirit took another step in her direction, slowly and methodically, as she continued to ramble on, blaming him for what she had done. Anna knew all the woman needed to do was show some sort of regret, some slight indication that she had a soul that had been darkened to some degree by her actions, but instead, Janice refused to accept any inkling of responsibility. Things weren't going to end well for her unless she changed her tune.

"I tried to make it work between us, sweetheart. You know I did. I took out a loan on the house to buy this place, but you couldn't see past the repairs. You were so angry about the loan, and I would have paid it back. Then you got so worked up over that little flirtation—"

The lights flickered, a handful of bulbs bursting into thousands of shards of glass overhead.

Janice yelped. "Okay, so I slept with him! That was your fault, though, and I told you that! A woman has needs, and you just didn't meet them. You refused to find a second job, and you refused to give me access to your bank accounts. I was the one suffering! Yeah, I might have pushed you that night, but you killed me long before that. You murdered my spirit, Neil."

Emily's eyes shot to Anna's, matching her complete dismay at how little Janice seemed to care that she'd committed murder. From what she was saying to the spirit, it was becoming clear she hadn't been a good partner to the poor bastard for some time before his death. Anna desperately hoped for some sort of moral turnaround, some redeeming qualities in both women, but thus far, only Nancy has asked for forgiveness from the ghosts. It was reaching the point where a decision would have to be made.

The ghost wasn't going to stop, and she worried it would go too far.

As she started to stand, she felt something pressing on her shoulder. A chill ran down her spine when she looked up, body shaking to see a spirit resting his hand on her. It wasn't hard, nor did she feel as though she were in danger. He had to be in his late sixties, clad in pajamas with disheveled white hair and a scraggly beard. Anna didn't need a photo to tell her that the man standing over her was Claymont Harrington. He looked down at her, a comforting smile on his lips as he shook his head. Before she could react, he disappeared again, but the pressure was there, stopping her from standing or helping the woman at all.

"Janice, you have to show remorse. That's what they want," Anna said.

The woman's eyes snapped to her, a look of pure hatred evident there as she lurched forward. Once more, though, before she could attack, Janice was shoved backward by her dead husband's spirit. She slammed against the wall, and the wind was knocked out of her.

"You, you did this, you little bitch. This is all your fault…"

"I'm not a killer. That's all you, Janice. I'm trying to help you."

"You want me to apologize?" she snarled, her attention turning back to Neil. "Fine. Sorry, you were weak. Sorry, you didn't die sooner. Sorry, the only good you ever did was die so I could get your trust fund."

As her venomous words continued, the lights began to flicker. Between the seconds of plunging darkness and overly bright fluorescent lights, Anna and the others watched in horror as the spirits of Ryan and Claymont appeared again, joining Neil as he closed in on Janice. The woman's panic showed through for the first time, her harrowing screams filling the air as she begged for her life. One moment, as if it were being played on a flash screen, Janice was there cowering in the corner, and the next, she was gone, her haunting screams echoing down the hall. As quickly as it had started, the room became warm with the glow of the overhead lights again, and the calming atmosphere they'd created returned. Nancy was no longer sitting across from them but crumpled in a corner, her head buried in her lap as she whispered to herself over and over, rocking back and forth. Looking at her friend, Anna didn't know what to say.

"So…what now?" Emily asked.

She shook her head. "I don't know…but I do know we are finally free. The spirits got what they came for, and the house is ours."

45

"We found it exactly where she said on the video, Chief. It was buried for a good long time, but we should be able to get prints off the inside of the barrel where she grabbed it," the officer said.

The man nodded. "Good, let's get our men loaded up and get out of here."

The officer nodded and headed away from the front porch as the local police chief turned back to Emily and Anna. She could see the color hadn't fully returned to his complexion after watching the video footage they had shot in the room. That, coupled with the audio and Nancy's confession, was more than they needed to put her away for the rest of her life. It wasn't the murders bothering him. It was the unexplainable occurrences he'd seen on the videotapes that shook him to the core.

"Well, I guess that just about wraps it up for us. I'm going to be honest with you ladies. This case is going to be handed over to the state agency and possibly the Feds. They are going to want to talk to you again. I know I would. This is just too weird and way too far above my pay grade."

"Trust me, we understand," Anna said. "Honestly, we never expected this to happen. Where did you say you found her body?"

"Janice? Over by the creek. From the coroner's initial report, it looks like she died from a heart attack, but from what I've seen on that film, it sure as hell looks like she died from fear to me. Are you sure the two of you want to keep staying here? I can find you rooms in town at least till you get your affairs in order."

"We're fine, I promise. Nothing in this house is going to hurt us," Emily said.

"There is nothing left here to hurt us, actually," Anna said.

They both turned and looked at her, making Anna blush. She had always hated being the center of attention, but now, there was no way around it. The spirits had picked her to tell their story, and she owed it to them to follow through with it. Anna smiled and cleared her throat.

"They're all gone now. The only reason they were here was to get the truth. None of them could be at peace. I suspect that Nancy and Janice were the last of the Harringtons. As soon as they were gone, Claymont's spirit wasn't here anymore, and the same was true for Neil and Ryan. I honestly believe they've finally found peace."

"Well, this is going to be a media shitstorm. I can tell you that much. I'm happy I'm not the one who's going to have to deal with it. Now, I'm sure that you two will be getting better security around here before long, but until then, I'm going to keep an officer posted at the end of your driveway to keep away anyone who might want to get a peek at this place," the chief said.

As the man shook their hands once more and cleared out his men, they watched the hoard of officers, paramedics, and forensics personnel file back into their vehicles and down the driveway. When they were alone again at long last, they silently headed to the van, sitting outside in their makeshift outdoor kitchen, and popped open a couple of beers. For some time, they simply sat in silence, drinking and looking at the house in all its glory, until finally, Emily sighed.

"Tell me that all that just happened…it feels like a dream."

"No kidding," she muttered. "It happened, though, and the government has the tapes to prove it."

"Right," Emily said.

There was something about her tone that made Anna hesitate. Turning, she glanced at Emily, who had a playful and knowing grin on her face. Anna groaned. It was a look she knew all too well and, more often than not, caused her concern.

"Emily, what did you do?"

"Nothing illegal, I promise. They wanted the original files, so I handed them over…"

"And when the police asked if you'd made any copies? You know, copies of a confession in two active investigations?" Anna asked.

She shrugged. "Listen, I'm not going to do anything with them until this whole thing is closed and sealed off, but you can't honestly believe that the federal government is going to release those tapes at any point in time. Why would they? They've got a confession from Nancy, the gun she used to kill her husband, and Janice is dead."

"Then what do you plan on doing with it?"

Emily shrugged. "I don't know—"

"Bullshit. I know you, Emily. You always have a plan in place long before everyone else. So, fess up, or I'll send a ghost after you."

"Ha! All right, all right. We're not opening for a few months, and by then, the feds will have neatly swept this under the rug. I think that if those tapes happened to get released before the grand opening and there happens to be an added level of mystery to the mansion, it couldn't hurt our chances of having a booked-out bed and breakfast."

"Emily! You know there aren't ghosts here anymore. They've all gone. They're at peace now."

"So? The rest of the world doesn't know that. Plus, if you can get the word out there that folks can't get away with murder, don't you think that's what Claymont Harrington would have wanted? He wanted this place to be a beacon of hope, a place for people to come to rest their weary souls...but we've gotta have a hook to get them here, right?"

Anna shook her head but didn't shoot down her friend's idea, either. She loved Emily for constantly thinking one step ahead. As a pair of headlights appeared in the driveway, they both stood and waited to catch sight of the car. When they realized it was Lori's, the pair made their way over to her as she exited the vehicle. Emily pulled the woman into her arms, holding her in a tender embrace for a moment before letting Lori go.

"I got here as soon as I could," Lori said. "The police scanner said Nancy confessed, and Janice is dead? What happened?"

"Would you believe us if we told you it was the ghosts of Ryan, Neil, and Claymont?" Emily asked.

Lori's jaw dropped as she shook her head.

"Well, it's a good thing we've got proof then," Anna said.

As Emily laughed and the trio headed back for the van, Anna knew everything was going to be okay. They could once more sleep peacefully at night. As the others grabbed another round of drinks and Emily pulled out her phone to show Lori the video feeds, Anna looked back at the house. For a split second, she thought she saw Claymont Harrington in one of the windows, but the apparition was gone as quickly as it had appeared. She smiled and turned back to join the others. Perhaps the story of the Harrington estate wasn't done just yet, but there were more truths to uncover.

One thing was for certain. Whatever the world threw at them, they would face it head-on and together as a team. They'd overcome more than anyone could ever imagine, and Anna knew their story was just beginning. As with the estate, they were getting a second chance at life, and Anna wasn't going to waste a single minute of it. The Harrington story deserved to be told; it needed to be shared with the world, and Anna was going to be the one to do it. With a new goal in mind, she joined Emily and Lori. For just one night, Anna was going to relax, knowing that all was right in the world and that the Harrington sisters would never harm anyone again. The estate was finally theirs.

EPILOGUE

Anna couldn't believe the day had finally come. After everything they had endured at the estate, it was hard to fathom that they had reached the point where they could open their doors to the public. She wanted to believe that everything was going to go off without a hitch, but the last several months at the estate had taught her that anything was possible. Between facing a dozen unexpected problems, not to mention the murderous sisters, it had come down to the wire. There were places where the paint was drying that morning, but now, everything looks brand new and accurate to the time when the estate was first built.

Together with Emily, they decided on an evening grand opening. It fit with the theme of the haunting and the sordid past of the property. Since the arrest of the mayor and the town's financial advisor's death, the community had stepped in and taken a long, hard look at how things operated. At that time, more corruption and greed from the sisters had been uncovered. With them out of the way, though, the town had started to flourish. They had come together with Anna and Emily to make the estate a part of the fabric of their lives, something she knew Clayton Harrington would approve of. Despite being found mentally unable to stand trial, Anna knew they'd heard the last of Nancy.

She would spend the rest of her life locked away in a mental institution while the world continued to move around her. Glancing at her reflection in the mirror one last time, she took a deep breath and stepped out into the foyer. She saw Emily and Lori through the hordes of gathered people, staff, and media outlets. The official ribbon cutting was twenty minutes away, but the air was buzzing with anticipation. Lori squealed with delight as they embraced, Emily beaming with pride next to the pair.

"Oh my gosh, this place is packed, Anna! How excited are you right now?" Lori asked. "You know I saw Richard Fermont earlier… Can you believe it? The freaking *Fermont Press* is here!"

Anna didn't know what to say, but it didn't seem to matter as Lori continued to give her a complete rundown of everyone who was important in attendance at the gathering. What had started as a small and local event had ballooned as the story of the murderous Harrington sisters circulated the national news. It was good for the bed and breakfast, but it seemed like a dream to Anna. On occasion, she caught herself pinching her arms to see if it was all real. There was so much happening around them that she didn't know if it would ever sink in.

"...then over by the buffet, I saw Soren Peller, and she writes for the *National Press Foundation*. They never report on grand openings unless it's something huge, and earlier, I met with—"

"All right, honey," Emily said. Her voice was sweet and kind. "I think she gets it. There are a lot of people here."

Lori blushed. "Sorry, guys, I'm just so happy for you two. Seeing what you've done with this place is just stunning. I'm so happy you kept it original and didn't try to make it modern."

"Like you would have let us," Emily said.

"Plus, it's modern enough. We've got the best internet connections, chefs, and reviews out there, plus all updated amenities, but yeah, I'm happy we kept the aesthetic, too," Anna said. "So, I guess we should start heading for the big event, huh?"

"Don't sound so excited," Emily said.

Lori gave her partner a playful grin. "Trust me, I know just how she's feeling, and I'm not even the one in the spotlight. But don't worry, Anna, we are going to be right there with you the whole time. If it all gets to be too much, just say Chicago, and I'll drag you away from the masses."

"Ha! Our very own safe word. I like it," Anna said. "I suppose we better go give the people what they want. If you'd have told me this was where we would be a year ago, I would have locked you up in an insane asylum."

"It's hard for me to believe at times," Emily said. "I wouldn't change a single minute of it for the world."

As Emily exchanged a loving glance with her partner, Anna couldn't help but smile once again. They were a match made in heaven. She couldn't fathom how different things might have turned out if it wasn't for Lori. She was a perfect match for Emily in every way possible. It brought Anna an incredible amount of joy to know Emily had found her soul mate. Anna's own love life was on the back burner, and that was where she planned on keeping it. Just as Emily was passionately devoted to Lori, Anna was to her work and the growing business.

"Well, maybe being held hostage and all the gore… I think we could all go without that," Lori said.

The trio all laughed as a woman in a sharp black suit approached. It was one of the few faces Anna recognized. Whitney Heath was Anna's publisher. Her company was sponsoring the simultaneous launch of the bed and breakfast, along with Anna's first haunted mystery. Given the fictional novel's vast similarities to the Harrington estate and the events that had transpired, the book was already a hit. She couldn't wait to see what the future held.

"Well, I must say the turnout today is downright unparalleled. I haven't seen a hit like this in the last decade! Not since that last wizard book. Are you ready for the big debut?" Whitney asked.

She swallowed. "As ready as I'll ever be, I suppose."

"You're going to do just great, I know it—"

"Crap, I forgot something back in my room," Emily said. "Can you help me find it really quickly, Anna?"

She gave her friend a quizzical look. "Right now?"

"Yeah...please?" Emily asked.

Without hesitation, after promising a worried Whitney that they'd be right back, Anna jogged after Emily. As soon as they were alone, her friend spun around and closed the door behind them. She reached into her pocket and pulled out a small jewelry box. Anna couldn't hide the smile on her face as the tears started to swell in her eyes.

"Wh-what's this?" she asked.

Emily grinned. "Open it."

With trembling hands, she pulled the lid off the box. When she saw the white gold chain and pendant inside, Anna gasped. It was delicate and beautiful on its own, but the resin pendant captured her attention. It was her best friend's cherished blue glass, worn from her touch over the years into a smooth stone. A tear slipped down her cheek.

"Emily, I don't know what to say…"

"I don't want you to say anything," Emily said. Her friend reached out and picked up the necklace, opened the clasp, and slipped it around Anna's neck. "For most of my life, this little stone was my lifeline. It kept me alive in the darkest of times, but then I met you. You became so much more than just my friend; you became my sister. I wouldn't be alive today if it wasn't for you. This rock was the most precious thing I had until the day I met you, and now, I want you to have it," Emily said.

With the stone resting against her neck, Anna touched it delicately with her fingers as Emily came back around to face her. Emily reached out with a tissue, wiping away her friend's tears before pulling Anna into her arms. As she held her best friend, Anna's heart felt like it was going to burst with love.

For the first time in her life, she felt what it was to have a family. A moment later, there was a knock on the door, and they pulled apart. With matching smiles, the best friends emerged, ready to take on a brand new adventure.

Made in United States
North Haven, CT
24 November 2024